I0538645

NAMELESS, BLAMELESS REPRODUCTION

BY JACH MD

ISBN: 0615772056

ISBN 13: 9780615772059

Library of Congress Control Number: 2013903610

CreateSpace Independent Publishing Platform

North Charleston, South Carolina

This book is dedicated to women who have suffered
with either infertility or unwanted fertility,
and to their dedicated obstetricians and gynecologists.

PART I

THE INFERTILE OBSTETRICIAN

Assistance

Blog, People for Stem Cell Research:

I need help. I really need some help. [I hope this is the right blog for stem cell transplant questions.]

 I do not want to give my name or too many details, just an outline of where I am and why I need help for my infant daughter.

[I may ramble a bit, but no names, no places, and no times will be given.]

***

When I get the call, I just know. Can I just answer barely awake and go back to sleep, or do I need to be up in a flash? Some of it is the intuition that comes with getting calls in the dead of the night over many years. It's the languid pace of a person's voice with a bothersome question, the timid entry phrase, "I'm sorry to bother you with this..." Or it's the fear and panic in the voice of the person on the other end of the line, the short demands with panting in between.

The phone rings at 3:00 a.m. The caller says, "We need you in OR four, *now*!" I don't bother to ask. I just slam down the phone, and I'm awake. In an instant, I'm in OR four.

I'm called to assist with a cesarean delivery. In forty seconds, the baby is delivered. The other obstetrician and I close without saying much. We close and inspect every layer in detail. There's a steady flow to closing

1

the patient's abdomen. I'm a little tired, but each step prompts another, and before long we are at the skin. Afterward, the doctor thanks me for helping, because it can be hard to find help on a case, "You know, given the mother's condition." I just nod. This doctor is known to take the moms with HIV.

***

Blog, People for Stem Cell Research:

She has HIV. She was born with HIV. You may think that not many babies are born with HIV these days. There are so many treatments, and the rate of vertical transmission has dropped significantly, but sometimes it all fails.

[If you do not understand vertical transmission, you likely cannot help me.]

***

I am barely asleep when I hear the code blue alarm. I am up again. "Code Blue ICU...Code Blue ICU...Code Blue ICU..." rings out overhead.

I get to the ICU. There's already a multitude of staff at the bedside.

The same thin female is intubated. The anesthesiology team is managing the ventilator. She has a blue hue to her skin, and even with the endotracheal tube in place, her oxygen saturation level is not coming up. There is some pink frothy fluid coming up from the endotracheal tube. She's given fluids and furosemide, a powerful diuretic. The oxygen is set at 100 percent with positive end expiratory pressure to help keep her lungs open. The pink frothy secretions once coming up her tube with each expiration are now slowly retreating with each inhalation. One team member tries to suction some of the secretions. Her hematocrit and labs are checked. Her chest X-ray looks a bit like a snow storm with opaque, fluid-filled areas.

There's a bit of panic with the chest X-ray. This is an HIV-positive patient. She's just had a cesarean. With pregnancy and her HIV, her immunity is low. This chest X-ray could represent diffuse inflammatory changes of *Pneumocystis carinii* pneumonia (PCP), the flu, or maybe tuberculosis. A nurse has a box of specialized masks she's handing out to the staff to offer protection.

Oh God. Please don't let it be tuberculosis; I don't need to go through that testing again. We have all been exposed at some point; I feel certain of that. TB, the great white plague, which has baffled physicians for millennia, is still thriving today. Someone is keeping a record of all staff present, and if TB is found, we will all be hunted down. That will result in a few trips to Employee Health and Risk Management. There's an oxymoron; the only way to not have risk of infection at a hospital would be to not admit patients. Either way, Risk Management will track down everyone exposed. They will test for exposure with a purified protein derivative (PPD) injected in our forearms. If a person has been exposed, the area will become red, which is a conversion to positive. I am lucky that my PPD has not converted to positive. I haven't gotten TB yet, though lice, ringworm, scabies—well, let's just say those still get around. Suddenly I want to leave, but I don't because I feel the obstetrician might need some support.

Usually I'm called to help with emergency cesareans or postpartum bleeding. In this case I am almost superfluous. I see the patient's obstetrician. His patients often have HIV, hepatitis, and/or drug addiction. Many obstetricians would see his practice as a practice from hell. I go over to him. Through his white mask he says she has HIV, and she is not compliant with her medicines. Apologetically he says he hopes she has PCP and not tuberculosis.

I'm there the rest of the night and early morning. Despite the team's best efforts, the staff cannot get enough oxygen to the patient. Her heart races and falters. Eventually she dies.

It's always hard to see someone so young perish. When things happen so fast, sometimes it's hard to know what happened. In this case it could have been pneumonia or a pulmonary embolus. Even the flu causes many maternal deaths each year.

The patient is covered. She was so cachectic, so malnourished, for a recently pregnant mom; looking at her you would not have thought she just had a baby. As the team was working on the patient, her obstetrician did say she had used drugs, but she had stopped the hard stuff and just kept to the softer stuff with her pregnancy. I would think that meant she stopped the cocaine and just used marijuana.

I think almost any woman knows she shouldn't do cocaine in pregnancy. Cocaine can cause the mom or baby to have a stroke or cause the placenta to sheer off. Pregnant moms doing cocaine often come in bleeding, usually right around twenty-eight weeks, with the baby in distress and the mom needing an emergency cesarean. Certainly keeps our neonatologists busy and a little twenty-eight-week baby in the NICU can run up a seventy- to eighty-thousand-dollar bill. I don't think cocaine was this patient's problem, and she was not that premature. I really don't know how many weeks pregnant she was or much about the case at all. The baby we pulled out was four, maybe five pounds. If I had to guess, she was roughly thirty-four weeks, but then given how thin the mom was, I suppose the baby could have been very small at full-term.

I didn't notice any tracks, but a woman that thin may have been a morphine addict. Opiate addiction would be a plausible reason for her ultra-thinness.

But then she had HIV, so she may have wasted away given her disease, or maybe she just didn't eat enough. She seemed to have a lung infection, maybe HIV related. How sad if she just wasn't together enough to take the medicines she really needed. Maybe she was just suffering with depression and taking medicines for HIV was a painful reminder. How many people with HIV suffer with depression? I'd guess more than half, maybe upwards of 90 percent, or even 100 percent.

"She was in her early twenties, a college student." I hear this from her obstetrician, who sighs and says, "Oh God, I don't even know whom to notify."

He starts to open up with a running medical biography as I get on the computer to see if her admission data shows a next of kin. I am unable to find any such information. The charge nurse says she will see what she can find in the patient's personal effects. It's still quite early in the morning, and as we wait for the charge nurse to return from the locker room where the patient's items are being held, we decide to visit the baby.

Esquire

The business is attached to a townhome on the first floor. The only signage is a small plaque with his name followed by "Esq.," just above the doorbell. I would have never found this man, but he came recommended by my brother. A little nervously I ring the bell. I hear some barking and a high pitched, "Coming!" There is some scuffling and a door slammed, likely to contain the dogs. He opens the door. He is a rotund man with a pleasant, happy demeanor. He has a wide face and a wide smile to match. His dress is as radiant as his smile, a gold lamé shirt, mostly unbuttoned, with black shorts exhibiting the true meaning of shorts. His legs, almost revealed to the groin, are rather thin. He wears black sandals adorned with gold beads. This portends to be an interesting meeting with a lawyer.

He states my name as a question, to which I nod. We exchange the usual words of meeting and greeting. And he says with a flowing gesture, "Won't you come in?"

There is a small entryway; each wall is painted a different shade of green, from yellow-green, bright lime, emerald, to forest. On the dark forest green wall there is a huge white canvas with drips of all the different shades of green. The signature is large and illegible to me, but it takes up about a quarter of the painting. Above me is a green glass chandelier with white flowers. The bulbs illuminate from each flower, and odd glass monkeys seem to be attached to some of the flowers. The little creatures almost seem to be playing a game of hide and seek. Creatures or monkeys or what?

"Come this way."

We pass a small bathroom and enter the back office. Did I see a hot tub on the other side of the bathroom?

I wonder if I am showing too much interest in the surroundings.

The office is painted purple and red. I'm always amazed how certain shades of colors that I'd expect to clash can be tastefully chosen. The artwork of dogs has equally bold colors. There is a large, dark wood desk with two chairs on each of the longer sides. Through the glass top, there are two embedded computer screens facing each set of chairs, a clever setup.

He motions me to sit opposite him. Using my brother's name, he states that he is a nice guy.

"My brother?"

"Ahhh, that's the connection. You are not gay!"

"Um, no." I guess he didn't know he was my brother. I wonder what my brother told him.

He leans back in his chair. Looking perplexed, he rubs his eyes and then he opens them and gestures into the air like a Shakespearean actor, exhaling slowly, and says, "So you want to adopt a child with HIV?"

"Yes, a little girl." I pause briefly. "Have you helped in these situations? I was under the impression you had."

"Yes, but mostly gay couples."

"Is there a problem?" I add.

"No, not at all." He flexes his hands, palms toward me in a flapping gesture. He crosses his legs and leans back, eying me cautiously.

"The social worker I spoke with made it sound like there was a waiting list for such children."

"Huh?" He startles as to almost fall out of his chair.

"Children with disabilities," I clarify.

"Oh yes"—he rolls his eyes—"disabilities like Down's or CP. Sure, those kids are in demand. But not HIV, not hepatitis—I mean, those kids have cooties, right?"

I look puzzled.

He continues. "Well, you see, mental retardation, Down's, CP—those kids come with extra benefits and lifelong disability or subsidy checks. And retardation is not contagious, hmmm?" He chuckles lowly. "Well, that could be debated."

I give a polite chuckle. For a first meeting, he has a bit of a social charge.

"On the other hand, kids with HIV have lots of medical expenses, and well, people are still afraid. Yes, there will always be a fear of HIV." He takes out some paperwork and flips through the packet. He's distracted only momentarily, and then he focuses on me again. "You know, I'm proud of my community, stepping up to adopt so many of these kids. Of course, in some cases it's the only kids they can get. Either way, the gay couples I know are some of the best parents. They love unconditionally." He says this while pointing a finger at me. "And most of them have resources, so it's not like they are taking these kids just to get resources!"

"I'm sorry; did you say lifelong disability? I thought—but aren't mentally handicapped kids a lot of work? Don't they have medical expenses too?" I have some disbelief that he would broach a potentially offensive topic like this.

He waves his hand in a wildly outrageous gesture of *no*. "Most services are paid for lifelong by Medicare. You know. You're a medical doctor, right? Well, Doc?"

He continues, "You would be surprised how many people would rather raise such a child than take a job. In fact, some people try to give birth to disabled babies in this country. You're an OB, or rather an obstetrician, right? You've probably seen it." He nods and points two of his fingers at his eyes, which are bulging.

"I am an OB, but what? Seen what? People *try* to have disabled babies?" Doesn't he worry I may have misgivings?

"Uh-huh, the coke babies," he says and winks as if we are on the same page.

When I return a perplexed look, he continues.

"Moms know coke is bad in pregnancy." He leans in and whispers, "Even stupid ladies with little education know not to take coke in pregnancy. And sure some are addicted and they continue because they can't stop, but I think there are a few moms who take it to have their preemies. And...if they time it right, say twenty-seven to twenty-eight weeks, well, there's a good chance of survival, and they're premature enough that the poor kids will have deficits... like deafness, blindness, CP. Well of course, I don't have to educate you about the risks of premature delivery."

Silence.

"You look stunned. You don't believe it?" His fingers flutter through the air like a magician.

I am stunned, and yet I have an idea of what he is talking about, a sense that what he is saying might be true.

I always think it's strange when a woman who delivers prematurely wants to see the social worker before she wants to see her baby in the NICU. I remember one lady who left the hospital without ever seeing her baby in the NICU. When the NICU nurse went to see her before she left, the lady just told the nurse to call her when she needed to come pick up her baby, almost like she was waiting for a pizza order. I remember a candy striper asking the nurse if she thought the lady had post partum depression and the nurse rumbling something under her breath about wanting the benefits without really wanting the baby.

I must have had a look of disgust on my face, because the lawyer almost pleads with me, "No, really. I'm serious, and others maybe break their baby's fluid bag early, huh?"

I am pulled back from my tangential thinking of how those moms, if this is all true, are no better than the beggar moms in India who purposefully deform their children to make them better beggars. Oh, I really do not want to think about this. I look up at the ceiling and think silently to myself, "How did I get here?"

"I'm sorry. I am digressing." He leans back again. "So you would like to adopt a baby girl with HIV. Usually I discuss with the parents all about HIV and how it's spread, the treatment, and all of that. But, you are a doctor, so I won't go into all of that." He throws his hands up, "And, seriously, gay couples are pretty smart about all that stuff too."

"I will warn you," he continues, "I usually help gay couples, one or both gay men who may have breeder instincts. I have been told maybe I have some of those instincts and maybe that's why I help so many of these couples." He straightens himself a bit. "Oh no, I do not have any children myself, except my cute little poochies," he says in a higher tone and cups his ear, anticipating a response.

Surprisingly, as if on cue, I hear whimpers.

"Anyway, does any of this turn you off? You could find another lawyer, but I want you to know I will work to help you." A little softer he says, "And a gay brother, I figure you're okay with—" He abruptly stops. "Um"—he almost looks red—"you do know your brother is gay, right?"

"Oh yeah," I nod, and we both laugh.

Shrugging his shoulders he asks, "Would you want a different lawyer?"

He makes me feel a bit uncomfortable; he is inappropriately frank. There is a part of me questioning the whole situation, but I respond, "No, if you can help me, that's all that really matters." Although I am uncertain, I add, "I think you'll be all right."

"All right," he repeats with a hint of disappointment. "Let me show you my diplomas and certificates." And with this, the screens in the table light up and he goes through a mini-slide show of diplomas and state certificates and such. He also pulls up our agreement, which he goes over on the screen, and then he prints a few pages for me to initial and/or sign.

Once these are signed, he straightens them into a stack that he sets aside. Then he turns his full attention toward me.

"Please tell me." He pauses. "How does a forty-three-year-old single, female doctor decide to adopt an HIV-positive baby, anyway?"

Wow, there's a loaded question. Will I have to tell him about my life? How do I sum it up, and how much does he need to know?

"This is confidential, right?" I ask.

He looks dubious and almost insulted. "Yes, of course, and seriously, if you can, tell me anything shocking—"

I cut him off. "Look, I'm not in this for the wrong reasons. At least I don't think so. It's just my life is so personal, so…" I am uncertain what to say.

"When people start defensively, I wonder what they are hiding." He sings "hi-ding." His eyes brighten and he looks upward. "Why don't you just tell me your reasons?"

I think about where to begin. The marriage? No, not the marriage. Okay, the marriage. My brain runs through a flurry of images and episodes of my life. Some of them are difficult times, and I rush through them as if fast-forwarding my least favorite part of a movie.

I married a fellow physician. We met during our residencies. Our training consisted of endless work weeks, eighty to one hundred plus hours. I don't think there was much chance for outside socialization, and there were several resident marriages during our years in training. Residency is such a strange time. You get some respect as a doctor, but you are still young and learning, the perpetual student. You meet someone who understands your predicament and offers brief bits of joy away from the chaos. The proposal seems more like a promise, that if we can pull each other through this, then we can manage anything. The time goes very slowly, as if you will never be out of training, but then one day it comes to an end. You look back, and it is all a blur.

He was a pediatric resident. We met while rounding on infants. OBs, pediatricians, pediatric surgeons, and occasionally urologists split up the circumcisions of the newborn baby boys. The nursery has a schedule to divide the duty, and we overlap so that one group has done them, and another might be new at the procedure. "See one, do one, teach one" is an old medical school adage. When we met, he was teaching, and I was seeing. Not all baby boys are circumcised; only the babies whose parents desire their sons to be circumcised. Step one is to make sure that the baby being circumcised has a consent signed by his parent on his chart. The nursery pulls those charts and the corresponding babies. Then the babies are actually lined up. Before pulling the boy from the bassinette, he is unbundled from his blanket, and we check the ankle band to make sure all the documents correlate. Pediatricians are often timid with their circumcisions. I doubt many continue the procedure after residency. The rest of us, the surgeon types, just get it done.

Strange meeting, I can still picture him sweating through the procedure of a circumcision, shaking and trying to instruct me how to do one. Then when it was my turn to do the procedure, I thought he would never let me finish. "Did you aspirate first? How much did you inject? That's not enough! Wait, that's too much? Don't angle the clamp so much that way!"

I gave him a glaring look.

To which he responded, "Watch what you are doing!"

I made a deal with him. "Look, it's evident you don't like this procedure. To me, it seems pretty simple and straightforward. If you can keep quiet, I'll do the rest of them." I thought he was going to lose it, but he managed to keep quiet, and I kept my part of the bargain too.

Afterward, he made some joke, that maybe you had to have one (a penis) to appreciate the fear of the procedure.

I thought, "Maybe you had to be one," but I kept that to myself.

Initially, I was not impressed, but then we kept running into one another. It was easy to make light of our first acquaintance with phallic innuendos. When people would ask us how we met, we would simply reply, "In training," and then we would giggle at our inside joke.

I know a couple who met at an autopsy; stranger things can happen.

I think we were happy once—exhausted, but happy. We both worked excessively, but we understood each other's lives.

After all of our training, we decided to start a family. We tried and we tried. When we looked into the problem, we had unexplained infertility, the worst case scenario. That means there are no reasons, nothing to be found and nothing to be fixed. In general, 30 percent is ovulation failure, 30 percent is sperm production, 30 percent is blocked fallopian tubes, and the other 10 percent is unexplained, the hardest to treat.

I tried ovulation enhancers, which made me moody and bloated, but yielded no pregnancy. Then we moved on to intrauterine insemination with hormones for me and nearly every-other-day vaginal ultrasounds to ensure ovulation had taken place. Impressions pass of cold tables, skimpy gowns, cold gel, angling probes, dark rooms, and black and white monitors. This was exhausting and frustrating.

Then we moved to the big ticket, in vitro fertilization. This was expensive and time consuming, mostly on my part. Injections and blood draws to add to and measure hormones, my muscles and veins ache at the memory. By now we were in our mid-thirties. They retrieved six eggs and made five embryos; hardly a good output. A woman in her twenties might produce twenty, even thirty or more eggs. We had two implanted and thankfully two took, twins! Wow!

It was truly amazing to watch them grow in my belly, a boy and a girl. They made it to twenty-two weeks, when unexpectedly I started to bleed and I felt a gush of fluid. Amid the waves of contractions, I was placed on bed rest, nearly upside down. I had an IV with magnesium to try to stop the contractions. With the heat caused by the medicine and being tilted head down, I could feel the blood rush to my face and a pulsing in my ears. How long could I possibly stay like this? My answer came sharply. They were born that night; nothing could stop it. I can still feel the entire experience: the waves of contraction pain and the forceful expulsions with the release from pain, but not from the anguish, not from the overwhelming sense of failure. Born at twenty-two weeks, they were too early, too premature to save. The boy died within minutes, and the girl died two hours later. I held them both. They were blue and cold with sticky, thin skin. My daughter made small gasps on my empty, sobbing belly. This was the longest, most desperate and horrible night of my life; tears, tears, and emptiness.

I wanted to do something. I'm a doctor, an OB; my husband is a doctor, a pediatrician. But we could do nothing. Their little lungs were too underdeveloped to accept oxygenated air. I had desperate thoughts of suspending my babies in liquid oxygen, putting tubes into their umbilical cords; they could swim and float, and their lungs would be full. Anything, anything, if I could have, I would have tried anything. I wanted to do something, but this was all just inner turmoil--desperate thoughts, unstoppable thoughts, futile thoughts. I just held them, and prayed and cried, prayed and cried.

We made arrangements for cremation. No, my husband did; I was not able.

One night my husband said he was glad they weren't twenty-four weeks, when they might have been saved only to suffer lifelong delays of respiratory problems, CP, deafness, blindness, feeding problems, communication problems, and possibly never potty training. He said the potty training part as the most horrible possibility, and as a bit of a joke. Did he really mean for it to be a joke? There was really no humor in it. Was he really glad our babies could not be saved? I was too empty to respond. In fact, I was too empty to respond to anything, and that's how the separation began. Two years later we divorced. I'm sure other couples find strength in one another after such a tragedy, but for me, I felt alone. Of course, the clincher is my being an obstetrician-gynecologist. I felt certain that I diagnosed more than the usual number of unwanted teen pregnancies in the following months; typical.

Maybe that's what doomed us: my life and my job. Some people may be able to drown themselves in their work; I think maybe my work drowned me and pulled me into lower depths. I often wonder how my patients didn't see it in me. Sure, I did my job, but I really had nothing to give them. Maybe they had their own joys and pains, and never really noticed me. My husband did notice, though.

We were civil until it came down to what to do with the remaining three embryos left over, frozen in time. He wanted to discard them or adopt them out to another couple. I do not think an infertility expert would have adopted out our embryos; I feel rather certain they would be more likely to adopt out embryos from a younger mom with a healthier response, so that left only their destruction.

In the end I was awarded the embryos, but I had to sign multiple waivers that he had no fatherly duties, obligations, or child support whatsoever, and further, if I ever used the embryos, he was never to know. The forms I signed essentially turned my husband into a nameless sperm donor.

When he moved out, the emptiness I felt was the same, except now it was more visible. Shortly thereafter, he moved to another state. Not even Christmas cards have been exchanged between us, though I did get a few from his family.

As I neared thirty-nine, I realized how tired I looked. Somehow, I began to exercise and pull myself together. I was lonely. I did not want to remarry, and I didn't see any prospects. Then the ache set in, a baby. Oh why does this happen?

I went back to my infertility doctor, who made me go through counseling and a full psychiatric evaluation. I had resolve and I felt he was wasting my time, and my biological clock didn't have time to spare. But there seemed to be no other way around it, as my embryos were locked in a freezer under his key, so I saw the counselor and the psychiatrist. I often wonder what they thought of me. They tried to offer advice and counsel, but how many cases like this had they seen? Could they seriously keep me from using my own embryos? Other than talking me through my thought process, what influence did they have? They questioned if I had thoroughly thought this all through. Didn't they know I had thought it through? I may be single, but I have a good job, and I can hold my own. I told them I had, but in reality, nothing could have prepared me for a procedure to take on an embryo with my nonexistent ex-husband. His presence—I couldn't really feel it, but I wanted to. I tried to remember better times, and yet there was mostly...nothing, nothing but coldness, distance, and work.

So I went through the shots and the ultrasounds, alone. I was older and, I hoped, a little wiser. Of course, given my twin tragedy, I only had one embryo implanted at a time. If one took, I would need to see a high risk obstetrician and maybe get a stitch in my cervix to help keep it closed until I delivered at full term. I hoped this time that would all come true.

I didn't tell anyone, not even my family. So when the first embryo didn't take, and the second didn't grow after thawing, and the third miscarried at seven weeks, I grieved by myself. I wondered what was better, having frozen embryos and thinking there's still a chance of having a baby, or knowing I've used my resources that they had a chance at life and no one is frozen in time waiting for a chance that may never happen.

This all seemed so unfair, and I cursed my fertile population of patients, especially the ones who were sad to be pregnant. I especially cursed the woman who bled so much after her seventh child that I was willing to forgo any payment (as she had not signed the correct paperwork in advance) to tie her tubes, because the next pregnancy might be too risky, but she told me to go to hell, because each of her babies got her extra money from the government. Yeah, I curse that bitch! If that was a test of my character, then I failed, not that anyone would know but me. I can remain cool on the outside amid my inner turmoil.

I often wonder why I didn't tell anyone. I know it's partly because I'm not that close to anyone. I know it's partly because I didn't want anyone to pity me. I also know that maybe I couldn't let myself get too hopeful; maybe I didn't really expect a pregnancy to take. All those years were a bit painful and I do have some bitterness, but I'm glad I never told anyone about the last three embryos. Even though I have no one to cry to, I also do not have anyone constantly asking me if I'm okay.

How do I sum this up for the lawyer? Something like, I was married, and we had infertility problems. We exhausted all of our resources, and we divorced. I have been managing on my own for a while, and I've thought about a child.

When I realize that won't be enough for this lawyer, I open up with the whole story.

The lawyer is a good listener, but eventually he asks, "Are you okay?"

"Yes, I think so." I guess I had that coming to me.

"Does your brother know?"

"He knows we tried to have a baby and that we split. No one knows about the embryos after the divorce; well, except now you know."

"It's just that I bet he could be a great support for you…I mean, you know he lost his partner some time ago. I think he's capable of—"

"Yes, I know he lost his partner." I don't mean to sound blunt.

"But he knows about the adoption, right? He sent you my way?"

"Yes, believe it or not, we are fairly close." I don't get to talk to my brother all that much, but I am always glad when I do. "And he told me if he was ever to adopt, you...would...." It suddenly hits me. How does my brother know this lawyer? Was he ever interested in adoption?

He smiles. "Your brother is a gentle soul." And that is that.

The lawyer recomposes himself. "So you are looking for a child to add meaning to your life. Or you feel alone and you want someone to depend on you."

"Was that a question?"

"No, well, I am just trying to put it together." He folds his hands. "I mean, if you want a child, why not just go through an agency or become a foster parent? I mean, why this child? Why the rush? Why a child with HIV?"

"Oh, right, well," I begin to describe this to him. "I guess I feel a connection to this baby." Why the rush? I am forty-two—no, forty-three. Oh hell, he knows that. "I'm sure if I had to start from scratch with an agency and all of that, I could. It's funny; I've never really considered adoption before this. I am sure I could love any child, but I feel I was thrown into this scenario, or rather into this child's life, for a reason. "

"I see. Tell me how you have a connection to this baby. Did you deliver the infant? Did you know the mother?

I have to think about how I got so involved in this case.

"I was called to the delivery to help with an emergency cesarean. So I guess I did help deliver the infant. I did not know the woman prior to the delivery. She had a bad pneumonia, and her lung function was deteriorating. She was becoming hypoxic, meaning she lacked oxygen, and the baby didn't tolerate that well. The baby's heart rate dropped, and an emergency cesarean was indicated. I was the OB in the hospital that night, and I was called in to help. It was about three a.m., and the patient was already under anesthesia for the surgery by the time I came into the OR. She endured the operation. Often after delivery, women with pneumonia will get better, but in the recovery area, the woman's situation worsened. She couldn't be stabilized, and she died." I think, "Luckily, it was probably not tuberculosis."

"I was up most of the night with the patient's OB, and we went to see the baby, who was stabilized in the NICU. The infant was almost thirty-four weeks. She was four and a half pounds, a good size, considering all that her mom was going through. I mean, her mom was very thin, wasting away with very little muscle mass, maybe one hundred ten to one hundred twenty pounds while eight months pregnant."

I think to myself, when I first saw the baby, she looked calm. She was breathing under the oxygen hood; she didn't need a breathing tube. She was kept in isolation, given mom's medical problems, alone.

"The mom had quickly signed consents, very hastily at the time of arrival. She signed permits for medical treatment and cesarean or delivery, as all pregnant women do. She had also signed cursory permits for medical treatment of her infant, but given the quick nature of the cesarean and her demise, the neonatologist never got to meet the mom prior, so he never got to go over the more in-depth consents for treatment of the baby. Of course, doctors do whatever we think is necessary for stabilization. Anyway, at first, the overall consent would have to do for the baby, but for non–life-saving measures, which are somewhat open to interpretation, more consents would be needed." I realize I should try to summarize this a bit more, but I am not able.

"Usually in preregistration, women will designate a next of kin. Because she had come in a little early, she did not preregister. Well, honestly, I think she could have preregistered before her baby was due, but I don't think this was the kind of woman who did much planning. In fact, she didn't get a lot of prenatal care, and after her diagnosis of HIV, she had disappeared for a while."

To this, the lawyer gives an understanding nod.

"The social worker could not find any phone numbers, and the main obstetrician's office didn't have anyone on file. Well, actually, they had a friend's first name and a cell phone, but it was disconnected. They tried to trace some phone records, but...I really don't know how you do that, or maybe they didn't because it would be a violation of privacy. Anyway, there just didn't seem to be anyone to call that first day. The main obstetrician couldn't really remember her ever coming with anyone to the office visits. He said she was single and that she thought she maybe had contracted HIV from dating some ball player."

The lawyer seems to have all the time to hear the whole story, but then again, he is paid for his time. Still, I realize maybe I'm giving too much detail. So I leave out that the obstetrician was not certain what kind of ballgame this guy might have played, but I recall him saying, "God only knows how many ball players have HIV, and I'm not just talking pro players, even the high school and college guys seem to get around these days." That was news to me; I just hope his view is skewed by his patient population.

From all of my talking, my throat has become dry, and I ask the lawyer if he has any water. He opens a small refrigerator by his feet and hands me a bottle of water. I thank him, and I take a few sips.

As I'm trying to adjust my story, the lawyer finally interjects. "I'm sorry, isn't HIV a communicable disease? I mean, don't you have to notify some health agency about her status, and then they figure out who she may have been—" he holds up his fingers like quotation marks—"in contact with?"

"That's true, I am sure the HIV result was reported, but..." I pause to think.

"Well, don't they have to contact the person and all of her exposures?" More hand signals.

"Honestly, after I send in a form regarding an exposure and I put a copy in the medical record, I don't really know what happens from there. I also know she disappeared for a good portion of her pregnancy, so maybe she couldn't be reached. In any case, there weren't any exposures noted in her medical record." I signal quotes as I repeat his choice of word, exposures.

He delves on. "I mean, there has to be a father out there somewhere, right?"

"I know the father space was left blank on her prenatal records. I am not sure she knew who the father was. I know the social worker has been trying to find someone, anyone, who might be the father. Initially, there was no one to contact."

I remember her OB telling me that the patient never seemed to open up about her life and that, in retrospect, maybe she even seemed a bit afraid. She was late to seek prenatal care, and after her diagnosis of HIV came out, the patient missed many appointments and was unreachable. When she returned for prenatal care, he tried to get her to see a social worker or a counselor. I think he may have one permanently in his office, but I don't know what happened.

I even say this, "I don't know what happened. I think the first problem was that she arrived in the middle of the night. I mean registration workers are almost always around. They are usually there at the most inconvenient times. Even when a lady is screaming and about to deliver, they arrive asking her all kinds of questions about insurance and such, but there are not as many of them working in the middle of the night."

"Okay, so you are telling me this woman delivers a baby, then dies, and there's no one to notify?"

That about sums it up. "Yes, well, at first, and then as far as the baby is concerned, the hospital has a policy." I shake my head. "Or maybe it's a state policy—that if no kin can be found, that two doctors can sign consents until a court can appoint a guardian."

"And you were one of the doctors?"

"Yes, but only for a day or so. But it did keep me involved with the baby's progress."

"So who is the guardian?"

"The social worker did find a stepmom and a much younger half sister. The stepmom gave information that the patient's mom died a while back and that her dad died only about three years ago. The stepmom has no desire to keep the baby. So the social worker had to get a court-appointed emergency guardian."

"And do you know who the guardian is?"

"Initially, it was a woman lawyer who is involved in child advocacy."

"And now?"

"Well, it's the same lady, as far as I know."

"Do you know if this lady wants to adopt the baby?"

"No, I don't think so, but the baby hasn't even left the hospital yet. I mean, I guess she's still the guardian, but they're looking for foster placement. Or adoption, of course, which is why I am here. But I know that there is a process and courses to take and home inspections and all of that, so I really need to get this all going."

"Aha. And you are certain that this is the baby for you? Tell me what you know about this mother. She sounds like she...Well, I mean, drugs, diseases; the child could grow up with many handicaps and be a huge burden." He says *huge* holding his hands out as if to describe a large fish caught. Seeing my expression, he drops his arms and adds, "I do not like the word either, but you have to consider what you are getting into. And once you are in, you are in it for life if you adopt the baby. Maybe foster care would be a better start; it's less permanent."

I know what he is saying and that he is just covering all of his bases. That way, I can't come back and say he didn't counsel me well. But I am hard-headed, and when I decide to do something, I do not back down. I figure he already knows all of this with what he's heard from me already. "I don't know a lot about the mom, but I can put most of her story together. For starters, I know the mom was a college kid who probably pushed her luck and got pregnant. Reluctantly she accepted the fact she was pregnant, and she got prenatal care. Then I figure, she had another bomb dropped on her with the diagnosis of HIV, and she disappeared for a while. When she did return for prenatal care, she didn't take her medicines, the ones for HIV. I cannot say why. Maybe she thought they would hurt the baby." There's a sad statement. With antiretroviral (HIV) medicines, the chance of vertical transmission can be lower than 2 percent, but without them it can be over 30 percent. "I guess they can cause side effects, but truthfully I just do not think this woman was all together. She may have had some denial, and in this case, a pregnant woman finding out that she has HIV, I think she had to have suffered with some depression."

Again the lawyer gives a knowing nod. Depression is all too common in the HIV-positive population. My recent research shows prevalence over 60 percent, and probably that's a low estimate.

I continue, "I know she did some illegal drugs, but I am not sure which. All that I know is that her OB said she had stopped the hard stuff, so usually that leaves marijuana. I know he frequently does drug tests on his patients, but when I asked him about that, he said, 'Well, I do what I can to get them to stop.' Surprisingly, her preliminary toxicology screens at the hospital were negative, and in general the final reports never vary, but I don't know the final report." I seem to ramble on. "So she's not the birth mother I would have chosen, but the baby seems like an innocent survivor. Cesareans also cut down on transmission of HIV to the baby; I am hoping that since hers was done before any labor, there might be a chance that the baby doesn't have HIV."

He startles. "Wait, what did you say? The baby might not have HIV?" He springs to the edge of his seat.

"Well, she's not even a week old. The preliminary tests are positive, but we are waiting for final results, and maybe they are back. Even if they are positive, they may repeat them in a few months to be certain—"

He cuts me off loudly. "Ah, well, that could change this child's outlook for adoption considerably." He shakes his head in frustration. "I'm sorry; I'm a little confused. Didn't you say that the baby has HIV?"

"I think that she does, and the results might be back, but now that I am not the guardian—well, I never was the guardian, but you know—I am not overseeing the case, and so I do not have access to her records."

"Oh, well, why do you think that she has HIV?"

"She's still getting antiretrovirals. So I am guessing that she does have HIV, but honestly, I'm not one hundred percent sure, and really it doesn't matter to me."

"Of course, even if there's a chance of HIV, adoption can be tricky. Most parents would want a certain, an absolutely certain, negative before making any decision toward adoption."

Maybe he is humoring me, but he takes my case, and there are loads of papers to sign and appointments, classes, and meetings to schedule. I leave feeling that I have a good lawyer and counselor. I am making progress.

First thoughts of adoption...

Without any family to call, a social worker is called in that Sunday morning. She states that without family, two physicians can sign in agreement the consent for the baby's care. As there are not too many doctors at the hospital on Sunday morning, the other obstetrician and I, at the social worker and neonatologist's urging, sign the consent forms in agreement. Lines, tubes, transfusions, medications—I am surprised at the list of procedures that we consent for. I guess everything has risk these days.

I ask the neonatologist if the baby needs a blood transfusion. He says there is a good chance that she may need a transfusion due to lack of nutrition, and sometimes, after such a sudden birth with possible infection, there can be a delay for a few days for the baby to start making blood. I know many preemies need blood, but I wonder why they use adult blood to transfuse these babies. It doesn't make much sense to me to give a baby only 2 to 5 percent of a unit of adult blood and then discard the rest. Why not separate some units into ten mini-units for Neonatal Intensive Care Unit use? At least then, we aren't wasting 95 percent or so. Why not use babies' blood, blood obtained from placental umbilical cords at birth? This infant blood carries more oxygen than adult blood, and that might decrease their need for such high doses of oxygen. I know if I ask this pesky question, he'll tell me that they collect too-small amounts of blood from umbilical cords, but tests can be done on small amounts of blood. Why not give them umbilical cord blood, whole, which has better oxygen carrying potential, growth factors, and stem cells? The stem cells might repair injuries from prematurity. If a preemie received multiple transfusions with stem cells of different genetics, would the baby be a hybrid of multiple genetics? Would such a hybrid be good or bad? Better at fighting off infection and immune surveillance or worse? More immune tolerant or less? Would the baby turn into a super human who lives much longer or not?

Oh my, for such little sleep, I seem to have a brain surge, a mental tangent. I do not know why I do that, but that's the way my brain works. On this occasion, as I leave the NICU, I have to laugh at myself. I am such a curious individual, but during the dark periods of my life, following my fertile losses and my divorce, I remember my mind being so quiet, so routine and monotonous. It was like I was on auto-pilot. Now I am thinking again, and I am invigorated!

After this, throughout the day I am consulted here and there, and I need to be available to sign for care. This goes on for a day or two. I am paged with updates, and I go to the NICU to sign. The neonatologist meets with the other obstetrician and myself and discusses the baby's progress and what else she needs. The other obstetrician seems interested to know if they have found any kin or someone to take over guardianship, while I am interested in the care of the baby. I visit the baby with my white fitted mask and yellow gown. When I peer at the baby's big gray-blue new eyes and let the baby grasp my pinky, which is adorable even if it is just a reflex, why do I feel that she is reaching out to me? Somehow, I don't feel so alone, and I know that, if there is any chance, I will adopt this little girl.

On Tuesday afternoon, I realize the paucity of updates, and I go to peek in on the little girl. I find the neonatologist speaking with the social worker and a smart-looking lady, nicely dressed in pumps and a pencil skirt. The social worker sees me and breaks away to tell me she has "good news." The baby has a guardian now, and my help is no longer needed. Something to the effect of, "Thanks for helping; I'm sure you're glad you won't have to be bothered anymore." We exchange niceties, and I leave.

I feel like I was intruding.

I drop in to see the social worker the next day.

She has a very untidy office with piles of paperwork. I feel a little cramped.

"What can I help you with, Doctor?"

I am always bemused at the generality of being called doctor or doc, which is more often than not. "Well," I reply, "I was wondering about the baby."

"Yes, what about the baby?"

"Well, is there any family? Have you found the dad, yet?"

"Listen, I am glad you are interested, but I am busy, and I really can't tell you too much about the case anymore."

"It's just…" This is harder than I thought it would be to discuss. I figure it's now or never. If I am serious about this, I need to tell someone. "Um, I might be interested in adopting her or being her foster parent…I mean, if no one else comes forward." It just spills out.

"Oh, look, I am glad you helped when she needed the immediate care that she did need, but the court has appointed an interim guardian, and I am not sure what to tell you about what you are asking."

"I know you found a friend's number on the chart. Did you find any family? I mean, am I wasting my time even thinking about this?"

"Okay," she concedes, "the friend was just a first name and a phone number on the prenatal record from her doctor's office, but the line was disconnected."

I drop in to see the social worker the next day.

"But then didn't you tell me you were going to look at phone records or something?"

"Yes, but—I am not sure how much I can tell you."

"Does the baby have family?"

She looks at me squarely and then slowly starts to shake her head. "No, no one wants to take the baby."

"I talked with the patient's obstetrician, and he said maybe you found a stepmom? He said he found a number on the chart in his office."

She looks exasperated. "All right, yes, there is a stepmom, who has been difficult to reach, and she has made it quite clear that she wants nothing to do with the baby."

"Is this the only family you have found?"

"Yes." She gives in. "The stepmom and a half sister who is only six years old, or so. And the stepmom let me know that the patient's dad died only a few years ago, maybe three years ago, and her mom has been dead for quite some time." The social worker seems lost in thought for a moment as she recalls the countless telephone calls. She really had to work to get in contact with the stepmom, and when the lady thought there was any chance the social worker or the state would pin the new baby on her, she became very hard to reach. She hung up several times and then screamed at the social worker not to call her anymore and then hung up. All phone calls either went unanswered or went to a full answering machine. The social worker finally got a chance to leave a message that she did not expect the woman to have any child care duties or funeral duties; she just wanted her to answer some family questions and wanted to know if she knew of any potential fathers or kin. "What a mess!"

"Do you know about the patient's family? Why did her mom and dad die? Do you know?"

"No."

"The patient had health problems. Do you know if her—"

"No, I do not know." She cuts me off.

I drop in to see the social worker the next day.

"But there's no family for the baby, right?"

"No. No one wants the baby," she says abruptly.

"And the baby's dad, is there any potential?"

"Again, none that I know of," she blurts out.

"What about the guardian?"

"What about her?"

"Well, does she want to adopt the baby?"

"I doubt it; she is just temporary until we find foster care or a father or some other family, but I think the child will be a fost-adopt."

"A fost-adopt?"

"Yes, that's where the baby starts with a foster family who has the desire to adopt and knows that if a certain amount of time passes and no family comes forward, then the baby can be adopted."

"How much time?" I can tell she is becoming irritated by my questions, but I need to know.

"I am not really sure."

"So she is potentially adoptable?"

"Yes, but I wouldn't get your hopes up. I mean, couples can wait years to get a baby, and we are not sure that a father won't show up."

"But given all of the circumstances?" I ask, thinking of the mom's HIV status.

"Yes, even given all of the circumstances, people want babies, and believe it or not, they want them even if there are potential disabilities."

I must have a look of disbelief.

"Actually, some especially want babies with disabilities." Then she adds, "Look, just because you were available to sign consents doesn't put you at the front of any adoption list."

I find the disabilities issue hard to believe, but then I realize that I am certainly not immune to desperation, so why would anyone else be?

I drop in to see the social worker the next day.

I say, "Well, what would you recommend that I do, if I am really serious about a possible fost-adopt?" I am growing more comfortable with the new word.

"I would probably get a lawyer. And get a good one who specializes in adoption, and if possible, adoption of potentially disabled children to single parents, if there is such a super-specialization. And get references to make sure you get a good lawyer."

"Do you know any good adoption lawyers?" I inquire as my mind wraps around the fact that she knows I am single.

"No, believe it or not, I do not. Well, actually, the woman involved right now is a lawyer, and child advocate, but," she warns, "do not approach her."

"But haven't you had such cases before?"

"No, nothing quite like this. Most adoptions are arranged before the woman goes into labor."

"How long would it take if I got a lawyer?"

"I really can't say, but I know they will want a physical exam, and your financial information and a home inspection, a background check and parenting coursework and references. Are you married? I mean, you're not, are you?"

"No," I answer, and I think to myself, "but I thought you knew that already."

"Then they may also want a contingency plan, of sorts."

"Uh-huh. But about what time frame; do you think that I'd be ready by the time she's ready to leave the hospital?"

"Well, I've learned to 'never say never,' but I think it's highly unlikely. I mean, they may have already contacted an adoption agency and started to look at potential foster parents. And I do not know the policy on getting a private investigator."

"Why wouldn't you know if an adoption agency has been contacted? Don't you start that contact? And a private investigator; did you mean to say private lawyer instead of an agency?"

I drop in to see the social worker the next day.

"No, I don't contact adoption agencies, and yes, I mean a private investigator to look for a potential father. And I am telling you that you might want to get one. I mean, if it were me, I would not want to live in fear that someone might surface and claim my child. And, also, you will probably want to get as much family history as possible. This isn't a matter to be taken lightly, you know?"

Huh, I was not thinking about that. "I guess if you are a foster parent that would be the time to look into that."

"Maybe you should get a lawyer first."

"What about an adoption agency?"

"I may be wrong, but if you want this particular baby and you haven't done anything yet, then somehow I think a lawyer will be more time efficient, but I can't say that you're not just wasting your time."

"Do you have any idea what this will cost? I mean, a lawyer and a private investigator?"

She huffs. "No, but I do know that babies and kids are expensive, in general."

I get the point, and I thank her and graciously leave.

As I go home that evening, I am lost in thought, and I have no idea where to begin. I don't understand why the social worker said, "...they may have already contacted an adoption agency and started to look at potential foster parents." I thought *she* was the "they." If she's not, then who would have contacted an adoption agency? I thought she would know or might be able to help me. "If there's any possibility," I think.

Except for the money spent on my divorce and IVF, I have had very few expenses in my life. I live in a three-bedroom house. I still live in the house my husband and I dreamed of filling with a family. We bought at a good time, and I just can't see moving. I have everything I need here, and I am comfortable.

Or maybe I couldn't get myself to sell the house. I know for a while I couldn't get myself to do much of anything. Then there was the renewed hope of fertility. I suppose I thought there was still hope of filling the house with a family. But then the embryos failed. I hate to use the word—failed.

And now there is this hope. "If there's any chance," I think.

And I do the unthinkable; I reach out. I can't say what leads me to do this, but I call my brother.

My brother...

I admire my brother. He is always accepted for being himself. The term 'comfortable in his own skin' comes to mind, and if there ever was adversity, he shrugged it off. Tensions never escalate around him, the definition of cool. I guess I figured out enough over the years watching his mannerisms. It wasn't obvious right away that he was gay, but over time it was apparent.

He's tall, lanky almost. He is always well groomed and well dressed. He's handsome in an overly clean fashion. He never had to tell me, and I would never have asked. Later in life, he introduced me to his partner, matter-of-factly.

When they lived nearby, I used to visit them. I was in medical school, and it was the best thing for a struggling student to go over and get a home-cooked, or rather, gourmet meal. That kept me coming over. It was fun, and we were all pretty close. Then they moved out of state. I was finishing medical school and then starting residency. I missed the conversations we would have, but I was certainly busy enough. He came to my wedding, which coincided with my graduating from residency.

His partner died shortly after my divorce. I didn't make the funeral; I was still in a cold, dark place. I feel badly for that. I always wonder how I continued to work through it all. I've never taken a break. I did change jobs, just once. Sometime after the divorce, I closed my private practice and became a hospitalist. The hospital where I work decided it would be a good idea to keep an obstetrician in the hospital for emergencies in labor and delivery, essentially shift work. I wasn't really certain if this was the right choice for me, but I jumped at the chance. I felt like maybe I could be less emotionally attached to my patients and just help out other obstetricians with their patients. But then, was I ever emotionally attached? Envy is an emotion, but it's not very binding.

In truth, patients deserve a doctor with a bit more empathy, and my calculating mind is probably better with emergency situations. Whatever the reality, it's been a good change for me.

My brother is one of the only people I confided in during the divorce and then the job change. We have had many long telephone calls. He always offers good advice. I know he has had many problems going on in his life, but he never really escapes his role as a counselor. I always feel like I am talking about myself. I hope I have helped him some, on the rare occasions when he has told me about his life. We have shared ideas and theories about HIV.

Interestingly, my brother never contracted HIV. At the time it was unclear as to why. He did say, at the university hospital where his partner was being treated, the infectious disease specialist was very curious about these cases of HIV-discordant couples. The physician drew my brother's blood, several times, mostly to monitor his HIV status. When my brother never seroconverted, or became HIV positive, his case became more interesting. As more and more of these HIV-positive/HIV-negative couples became apparent, the concept of a natural immunity grew. With my brother's consent, the doctor tested his blood to see why he naturally resisted the HIV infection.

My brother lacks a receptor, known as chemokine receptor 5, or CCR5, which HIV uses to gain entry into cells. CCR5 is like a lock to which HIV has a key. Without this one molecule on the T-cells of an individual, the HIV cannot replicate within the host. Possibly as much as 1 percent of Europeans completely lack this receptor, and lesser amounts in other ethnicities. I wonder what the chances are that I also lack the receptor.

In one of our late-night conversations, I asked if he thought there might be a way to coat this receptor with antibodies and hide it from the HIV virus in affected hosts. This way all of the little "keyholes" of the locks would already be full. Would this keep the virus from spreading to unaffected T-cells in an

HIV-infected individual? I guess as an OB, I am just thinking of how we protect moms who lack the rhesus factor on red blood cells from potentially reacting with their baby's red blood cells. We administer an antibody to bind up any possible rhesus factors, or Rh factors, on baby cells that manage to get into mom's circulation. These antibodies can circulate and last twelve weeks. Could we make such antibodies to bind up the CCR5 receptors, or could we make molecules of the receptor to bind up the HIV and prevent it from getting into the T-cells? Now the HIV "keys" would be surrounded by artificial "locks." When I tell my brother my theories, he calls me a geek and tells me not to think so hard. He is always more concerned about the well-being of others. He would tell me to stop trying to solve the world's problems, but I like my mental tangents, my futile fun.

Every time he comes to visit, I ask if he might think of moving back, but he says his life is elsewhere and his current job as a counselor is fulfilling.

My brother answers, and as always, he makes time to hear me out.

I ask him how he has been.

He tells me he is doing all right.

He asks me how I've been.

I say, "Okay." With a little coaxing, I slip into the story of the delivery, the maternal death, and the baby, and then the social worker, the guardian, and my desire to be a mom.

He says he gets it. He tells me he has been a "big brother" for a while, and it's great to feel like you can help a child, even if it's just a small break from their routine.

I tell him more about my conversation with the social worker.

He says, "Hey, I know a lawyer where you live, where I used to live."

"Is he good?" I inquire.

"Oh, he's the best!"

"Do you have references on him? Do you know any happy families he's helped?"

"References...I might know a few. I guess you could ask him, but seriously, take my word for it, he's good! If I were ever to think of adopting, he is who I would want to represent me. Let me get his number for you."

He sets down the phone and disappears for a few seconds.

He gives me the number and then adds, "Do you want me to call him for you?"

"Uh, I don't know."

"What's the problem? You need a lawyer, quickly. I know he's good, and, yes, I know of some couples he has helped."

Couples, I think, and it dawns on me that the social worker said I should look for someone who specializes in single parents. Yes, this could work! I tell him, "The problem is that I should get several lawyers' names and references and choose carefully, but I really don't have time for all of that." I pause. "Luckily I know you and I trust your word regarding his expertise. I will call him tomorrow, and with a little luck, I will have a good lawyer to represent me!"

"I'll call him too, just in case it might help in any way."

"Thanks." I don't bother to try to fight him on this.

"No problem."

"Hey, if I need a reference, would you speak nicely about me?"

He laughs a little. "You bet, Sis."

"Just to clarify, you will tell them good things, and only good things, about me, right?"

"Yes, of course. Gosh, the only bad thing I can think about you is that you're a quiet workaholic, and sometimes you overthink things. You are a cute little brainiac who puzzles over everything."

"Um, just make it sound good, like I'm a cautious person with a good work ethic! That sounds better, don't you think?"

"Yes, got it. You are cautious with a good work ethic!" he says mockingly.

"Okay, good. Thanks again." Oh, thank you, thank you!

My brother…

"Hey, call me with updates, okay?"

"Yeah, okay," I confirm.

"Best of luck!" he says before hanging up.

Thanks.

Preparations...

I don't have HIV. She is adopted.

A complicated process, from the hospital to home...

As I am on a fast track to get this adoption, I have follow-up conversations with my lawyer, sometimes several times a day. I wanted a friend to do my physical, and he said no. But then I was worried that I might not get an appointment quick enough with just any doctor. My lawyer set me up with a friend of his who even squeezed me in after hours. The doctor was a bit surprised I was a female. He even made a joke that he thought maybe the name I had given was a stage name or prospective name or something to that effect. I realize there is an amazing network, simply amazing.

I have to pull together prior medical reports, including the psychiatric evaluation I had before trying to use my frozen embryos. Unfortunately, the adoption application has questions regarding psychiatric history, and my lawyer says it's better to be up front and get it all out there, as if you have nothing to hide. He has me fax a release of medical records to have them sent to his office. I fill it out and sign it. I deliberate having them fax the medical records to me instead of my lawyer, but I don't want to seem like I have any reservations. Part of me wants to know what's in the psychiatric records, but a larger part of me is willing never to know. As I return the fax, I think, "Oh, God, can all of that history be brought out in court? And just how many people are involved in this court process anyway?" Although I don't feel like I have anything to hide, I still feel so vulnerable!

I have to choose references for me and a contingency parent in case something should happen to me. This is a little frustrating. I think of the single women who easily get pregnant and are never asked for references or what their contingency plans are.

I guess it's good I didn't use my physician friend for my physical, as she is going to be a reference for me. And then there's my brother; he's already agreed to be a reference. Can he be my contingency person too? I didn't exactly ask him that. Even though it's really easy to talk to him, I still feel asking him to be my contingency parent might be hard. If he didn't live in another state, maybe I would even ask him to co-fost-adopt with me. Co-fost-adopt, is there even such a thing? I wonder if a sister-brother couple is better or worse than a single parent. Who gets to make that judgment?

Who else would think I'm fit to be a mom? What about my parents? They are in town, but somehow I do not want to involve them until I am more certain of the outcome. So for references, I'll stick with my physician friend and my brother, but a contingency plan—I'll have to get more specifics from my lawyer.

I have to get a financial statement together. In reality this is not too hard. I am one person with a home, a car, a job, and checking and savings accounts. I have medical, life, and disability insurance through my work.

I have to write a personal statement. I jot down some thoughts realizing this is the start of several hours of drafts and frustrations! I get on the Internet to see if there's any advice out there, and I find a blog history with some good pointers. There has to be a template somewhere, but I search and I search, and there's not an example anywhere. I can see why. In reality, I do not wish anyone to read mine either. I trudge along and five hours later, I come up with a page and a half, double-spaced statement. I set it down to reread it later. Sometimes that gives me a different perspective. It would be best if I had time to reread it in a few days from now, but I don't have that much time to spare.

I have a list of safety inspections for my home. Luckily I live in a one-story home, without a pool, and I don't own firearms. That cuts the list almost in half. Smoke detectors are working; there are only two of them. The water runs. My toilets flush. I have hot water, and it's at the safer 120 degrees because that's the way the house came and I don't know how to change it. Fire extinguishers: I have one and it's out of date. I'll put that on my list to buy. Window blinds can't have cords. Sadly, I know this is due to children having been strangled by such cords. Windows need to not open past four inches. I inspect the windows. The kitchen has the usual kitchen drapes. The bedrooms have drapes, and the sliding door to the backyard is bare of any window treatment. The windows do open, though I have never done this before. I remember some home file, and I search through information until I find the information about the windows. It turns out that there is a mechanism that will keep the windows from opening, or it can be adjusted to allow a small opening. It involves moving a plate held by a small hex nut. I don't have a hex set, but I have a drill with more attachments than I could ever imagine (items left behind by my ex). The drill is bulky against the window, and I have to angle it a little. I release the screws with the plates and replace them lower on the window frames. I have five such windows with two screws each, and I manage to strip four of the screws. All the windows are adjusted at least on one side. I take the four ruined screws and their plates and place them in a bag to get replacements.

The oven needs to lock. I look at the oven panel, and there is a button that says "lock," and in smaller print below is, "hold three seconds." I press this for three seconds and, remarkably, I am unable to open the oven. Wow, who knew?

I need an escape route with a written plan. I need emergency numbers posted. I take out some plain paper and jot a home layout, and then with a red pencil, I mark the exits. It's kind of basic, but I figure an infant won't really know what it means anyway. I open a phone book and get numbers from the front for the police and firemen. I find a number for poison control. I jot down my parents' numbers, a neighbor's number, and a friend's number. I find an old document frame, and I put my emergency exit route inside, and I look for a place to hang it. I opt for the main entryway. I can't think of ever seeing an emergency exit route in any other house I have ever been to—an apartment or hotel room sure, but never anyone's house. I post the numbers on a cork-board by the phone.

I need to lock away any harmful chemicals and any dangerous tools. I round up every possible dangerous compound or device I can find, and I put them on the table. I will have to put these in a safe place. I am not really sure what to do with all of the cleaning agents and random assortment of tools I have. If I put them in the garage, how will I clean up minor spills and wipe countertops? I can't imagine running out to the garage each time I need to wipe an area clean. My cabinets have knobs, and I have seen some kind of locking plastic contraptions—I put that on my list and ask at the hardware store. I have to conceal or cover trash cans. The list seems to go on and on.

I notice at the bottom are two possible handymen listed that will help for a fee; maybe I should have started there. I need to label food and dispose of old items. Open items should be labeled with the date they were opened. I laugh. I add labels to my list. I have an assortment of plastic containers and baggies that I can use. I really do not have much in the way of food, but I make an ef-fort, and anything I'm not sure of, I just throw away. I am about to go through my refrigerator, when it dawns on me that I do not know if or when anyone will come to inspect my house, so I'll just wait until I get that notice. Lastly, I need a bed or a place for the baby to sleep, and I've been told to get a new crib, even if I have to return it. And if that is too painful, I can just give it away.

Where to go first? I choose the hardware store. Fire extinguishers are kind of expensive, but I grab two of them. I hope that is enough. I am relieved to find a whole section of baby-proofing items. I grab cabinet locks, outlet cov-ers, corner guards, toilet locks, knob guards, a power strip cover, and they really add up in price. I go to look for these specific hex screws, and I have to ask someone to help me. The guy notices all of my baby safety stuff, and he commiserates with me. He makes a comment about having to go through all of that and those "little buggers of window screws" and how much fun it is to move them. I agree. He also notices my cabinet locks that are made to go around the cabinet knobs. He says that's a good choice and that I wouldn't believe how hard it is to install those little latches that go on the insides of the doors. I just nod, not really knowing what he is talking about.

He hands me a bag of twenty little screws and says, "Let's hope you don't go through all of them." I thank him and head to the checkout.

I can't help but wonder if he adopted a child, but I realize he may have made all of these safety efforts for any child living in his house.

I know I need to get a crib, and so I head to the nearest baby mega-market. I am a little anxious as I park, and my fears only get worse when I walk in the store. I am overwhelmed. I know I should ask for help, but I am afraid that I will need to give too many details, and I am not really ready for that. I could say that I've volunteered to get a crib for my sister or something like that. Volunteered? No, that doesn't sound convincing. The furniture section is in the back, and so I realize I have to pass by every aisle. A lady offers to help me, and I say shyly, "I would like to buy a crib."

She questions whether I want a bassinette or a crib.

I try not to look puzzled and ask for a crib.

"Follow me," she says, and we meander by aisles of formula, strollers, car seats, breast pumps, toys, play mats, and more, much, much more.

We get to the crib section, and I pick out one that appears to be made of dark wood.

She takes down a number. "That's a really nice crib, and they also make a matching set of drawers with a changer on the top." She looks at me expectantly.

"Oh, no, I just need a crib for now," I respond.

"Okay, well, just so you know, there's also a nice matching glider and ottoman."

"Thanks." I acknowledge.

"So, you would like the glider, or maybe—"

"No, just the crib," I clarify. I start to follow her, thinking that we are going to check out.

She takes me to the mattresses and asks me if I need help picking one out.

"Does the crib come with a mattress? Or is one recommended to go with that crib?"

"The cribs and mattresses are sold separately. The mattresses are standard in size, and you want it to fit snuggly; so when you get the crib assembled and place the mattress, check to make sure you can't easily slide your fingers between the mattress and the crib slats. If there's any problem, you can call us, but we carry good brands, and I have not had anyone call with any problems." Then she says, "This is a nice mattress. I used this brand." So I nod, and she takes down another number. She continues, "Now, what about a mattress pad and fitted sheet?"

I think, "What about them?" I say, "Um, I guess I'll need them." Did she say something about crib assembly?

"Right this way. Have you picked out colors yet? Is this for a boy or a girl?" She seems to be looking at my tummy.

I have the urge to put my hands over my belly to hide whatever she might be looking at. "Just answer the question, nothing more," I think. "It's a girl, and I am not sure about colors, but I don't really want pink."

"Here are the bed pads, and they are all standard white." It seems by luck, or maybe strategic planning, there's an empty cart nearby, and she grabs the cart and points to one of the pads. I nod and she plops it in the cart. "Do you want two of them, you know, so you can wash..." I nod, and another goes in the cart.

We hit the bedding section, and there are comforters, but she says quietly, "It's not really safe to put lots of covers in the crib, and definitely no bumpers." She nods very seriously. "Most of the fitted sheets are just plain colors. I would avoid white or light colors because of stains, you know?"

I pick out two sheets in lavender, and she agrees that they are pretty.

"Do you need laundry detergent to clean those in? You know, hypoallergenic?"

I am not sure what to think. I guess it wouldn't hurt to get detergent, but as I think this, I shake my head no. "I am going to wait on that."

"Is there anything else I can help you with?" We are strategically in front of a clipboard on the wall with tear-off pages of a checklist for "Getting Ready for Baby." I am now certain that I am not just lucky. She tears off a page and hands it to me.

I glance at the extensive list with oodles of tiny check boxes. Wow, do people really buy all of this stuff? "Car seat" catches my eye. I know you can't bring a baby home from a hospital without a correctly installed car seat. I feel certain that I should get a car seat, though I wasn't specifically told to. "Can you show me car seats?"

"Well, of course. Follow me," she says as she takes off, pushing my cart with the bedding. She stops at an open section full of car seats and strollers. "Now, as you can see, these car seats that are sold alone are really for more mature children that can hold up their heads. Are you looking for a newborn or about how old?"

"A newborn." I am thankful I can answer the question.

"Okay, so you know that they have to face backward?" she says nodding, and I nod too, but truly just out of instinct and not wanting to stimulate any unnecessary conversation. "You could just get a car seat, and it has to fit on a base, like this." She says pointing to one with a base. "Then, as the child grows, you can change the direction of the chair. Oh, and this is a nice one because it has these nice, puffy headrests, and the chair is long and has these slits to adjust the straps higher as your child grows." I am still nodding. "But if you ask me, your best bet is to get a seat that clips into a stroller. They cost a little more, but then if you were to buy a stroller and a car seat, it probably is all about the same." She starts heading for these very large stroller combinations, and I conformably follow. "Now, these are wonderful, but quite large— and how big is your car?"

I startle as I realize I have to fit all of this in my car somehow. "I just have a four-door sedan, nothing too large, but it has a decent-sized trunk."

"You don't have a truck or SUV?"

"No." And I hope she doesn't ask about the father's vehicle.

"Hmmm," she thinks aloud, "I would probably opt for something a little smaller then." And like a model on a game show, she uses her arms and hands to accentuate a littler model. "This one is small, and it comes with this little metal gizmo, and you see how you can open this metal frame with wheels," she says as she opens the frame, "and the car seat just snaps in like this," and she snaps in the seat, "and voilà! You have a stroller."

I note that the price is more than the larger versions.

"Yes, it costs a little more, but it is a real savior! Those car seats can be so heavy, and when your little one is asleep, you don't want to have to wake her and try to move her to a stroller. This is really easy and light and portable. Everyone who buys this loves it!"

I just nod, and she lifts a rather large box off of a shelf and balances it on the cart.

"You should really get a little headrest to go with that."

What do you know? The little headrests are hanging in such a convenient location! I am wavering. "Uh, maybe I can think about that. I mean, I'll get one later."

"Actually, that's a good thing to put on a registry. Can I help you put a registry together?"

I am suddenly uncomfortable. "No," I reply. Please don't ask why.

"Okay, so what else do you need?" she says, pointing to the list in my hands.

I glance at the list. "I think that will be all for now." I can see she's about to recommend something more, so I interrupt with, "I'm sure I will be back. What is your name? You have been really helpful!"

"Oh, that's so nice," she says and holds out her name badge for me to read. "What about a baby monitor?"

"No, I'm good. How do I check out?" I interject before she can continue.

"Let me help you because I have the numbers for your crib and your mattress, and I will call and get someone from the back to help you get them into your car. Just follow me."

I follow her to the cash register, and I try not to jump at the final cost of buying baby gear for a mere chance at having a baby.

Once I sign, she picks up the phone and relays what has been purchased to the back. Within minutes a man comes with a flat bed carrying a large crib box and mattress in plastic.

He follows me out to my car. He fits the smaller stuff in the back seat; the stroller box just fits in the passenger seat, with the seat backed as far as it can go. The crib and mattress go in the trunk, but they are partially hanging out. He has twine and scissors. He twines the trunk down. Then he places a strip of red tape along the exposed side for safety. He gives me a nod and a thumbs-up.

I am shocked. That was amazingly easy. As I drive home, I think there was almost a Disney quality to the baby megamart: streamlined, politically correct, and easy to purchase more than I had ever expected.

The warning call...

Ironically, before the home inspection, my lawyer warns me firmly, "The woman who will do your home study will not want a written personal statement, but she will ask you all sorts of questions. Remember to be polite! Be as polite as you can!"

I wonder if he has reason to suspect that I will not be polite. Actually, the fact that she does not want my personal statement that I sweated over for the last few days is almost enough for me to be impolite!

I say to the lawyer, "Are you telling me I did this personal statement for nothing?"

"No, not exactly, but she will not ask you for it. Instead, she will ask you bizarre questions and even rude questions. Just try to answer them as well as you can, and don't get upset. She does not ask questions to be funny, so do not think that she is joking about a question. Again, just stay calm and answer them as best as you can. Do you understand?"

"Yes." I think she must have upset some of his other clients.

"Let me give you an example. Do you have a boyfriend?"

"No."

"Do you plan on dating?"

"I am not sure."

"How will you make time for the baby if you are a working mom? Who do you plan to help with childcare while you work?" He inquires.

"I plan to take some time off from work, and I will look into childcare." In reality, I am not sure. I think I might get someone to live in with me because I work long hours sometimes.

"How will you discipline the child?

"I might have some reading to do, but I'll figure that out."

"Do you believe in spanking?"

"No."

"Does spanking excite you?"

"What!"

"Good response," he chuckles.

I'm horrified. "Did she actually ask someone that question?"

"No, but I just wanted to see how you would respond to an awkward question. Just trust me, she will ask you something that makes you uncomfortable. Be certain of it. She's known to throw some weird questions out there. I usually tell people that if you start to lose it, just do that old trick where you imagine her in her underwear or naked. Just do what you have to and stay calm. You can always take a moment to think about your answers; or maybe even tell her you hadn't thought about whatever she asked before and you will need a little time to think it over. Okay, so you got it?"

"You make her sound really scary."

"She can be, but just take your time, and stay calm. Don't be overly talkative or gushy."

"Aren't you supposed to say, 'No, she's really a nice lady,' and make me feel less anxious about this meeting?"

"She may be nice underneath it all, but she's just doing her job. If she advises placing a child with someone who turns out to be a nut job, her butt will be chapped. Ah, now that's something to think about. So, just remember she's just doing her job, and just stay calm. Okay?"

"Okay, I will."

"Great. She has your telephone number, and she will call you before coming by."

"Do you know when?"

"I think she said she would find some time tomorrow."

"Do you know when or how long it will take?"

"No, but I would allow at least three hours, up to five, to be on the safe side."

"But I work tomorrow."

"You will need to make some arrangement so you are available to meet her at your house sometime, anytime tomorrow. Oh, and can you get me all the outstanding paperwork by tomorrow morning?" He lists all that is missing. "You can just fax it all over; if I need any originals, I'll contact you and send a courier."

"Do you need my personal statement?" I hope he will say no.

"Yes, please send me all you have together so far. Actually, she will want your personal statement in your file, but she won't rely on it or ask you for it tomorrow. She likes to ask questions. Oh, you have looked over the home preparation and gotten all of that together, right?"

"Yes, I may have a few minor details to get together, but I'm almost there."

"There's no almost. Get them all done. If you need any help, let me know. I can even arrange a handyman to come tonight if you need."

"No, I have it together. I just need to clean up a little and put labels on my food."

He laughs.

I get off of the phone with him, and I arrange to change shifts with someone. That's one thing about being a single workaholic for so many years: there's almost no other OB in my area who doesn't owe me a favor. Thank goodness, it is easy to change shifts. Then I go into a frenzy to clean my home and make sure it is baby-proof. I throw out half of my pantry and half of the poisonous cleaning agents. I put the rest of the cleaning stuff on a high shelf in the garage.

Between the windows and setting up the crib, I think maybe I should have gotten a handyman. The crib mattress is set at the highest elevation. The mattress fits snugly. I wash one mattress pad and fitted sheet and place them on the bed. The extras, which I now question why I bought, and the car seat are in a closet. The crib seems a bit out of place, as there is nothing else babyish about the home. No teddy bear or blanket to soften the atmosphere, but I can't think of that right now.

I think I should go to a bookstore and get some baby care books, because I really do not know that much about baby care, discipline, or even adoption. I can answer lots of medical questions, and I know to place the baby on her back to sleep, but the day-to-day routine is a mystery. I do not know if I can even take a crash course this quickly, but I feel like getting out of the house will help me.

I go to a bookstore, and I am bowled over by the amount of material out there. I pick out five books on adoption. One is of the For Dummies series, and it's a definite keeper. Somehow those are always well written and easy to read. KISS, or keep it simple stupid, is a great philosophy, especially in a pinch. I sit there and read for a while. I am happy to read that there could be a tax credit to help offset the adoption expenses, but then again, I may earn too much to qualify. I learn I should keep a journal, and I might want to have some baby names in mind. I pick out a journal. Somehow I think it will be much easier to write a journal than it was to write that personal statement. Knowing that no one will be expected to read it, I can be more open and honest, but not too honest...just in case. Of course what is more honest than bringing out my psychological evaluation during one of the darkest times of my life? Is it even honest? I'd say it's more violating, but what do I really know. I've never read the evaluation myself. I was allowed to use my embryos after the evaluation, so the psychiatrist must not have thought I was completely depressed, but in reality how could he make the decision that I was unfit to use them? I really would have lost it then!

That psychological evaluation sort of has me spooked.

Next, I flip through a book of baby names, but I fear it's too soon for that yet. Somehow, I think a baby name book might jinx the whole situation. I look at discipline books, but they are mostly for older children. There are books on getting your baby to sleep, feeding your baby, and, finally, basic baby care. I whittle it down to three books and a journal to buy; I check out and head home.

I read until I become tired. Tired is an overstatement. I try not to panic, and I hope I can sleep tonight. I do not know if I can start to get my hopes up or not.

As I lie in bed, somehow I wonder what my ex-husband is up to, and if he would approve. I do not know why I ponder this. It reminds me of our embryos I tried to implant without him. That was a strange experience, and somehow I have a small sense of déjà vu, and I get a bit chilled.

And I know he's moved on.

The home study...

The home study social worker knocks on my door. I peer through the peep-hole, and my stomach does a flip. She wears slacks and comfortable shoes, but she has a militant stance. I open the door, and we exchange greetings. She comes in and takes a good look around her. I am faintly reminded of my first meeting with my lawyer.

She explains that she has not fully made it through my physical exams, personal statement and financial records. This is no surprise to me, as some of them I only faxed to my lawyer this morning.

She continues, "Honestly, those don't tell me what I really want to know, and I can tell a lot about a person by visiting with them and seeing how they live."

I offer her a beverage, and she declines.

"I have compiled a list of questions for you." She has a computer tablet that she opens, and then she delves right in. "You have a nice home. Do you have any pets?"

"No."

"Would you say it's a safe neighborhood?"

"Yes."

"It's a two- or three-bedroom home?"

"Three."

"Do you mind showing me around the home? I have a checklist of items I need to see."

We start in the kitchen, and to my surprise she picks out random items from the refrigerator and looks at dates. She inspects the kitchen window, which does not open. She sees the phone and the phone numbers posted. She scribbles on her work pad. She looks at the oven and notes that it is locked. She runs the faucet, and she asks where my water comes from.

"The city." I guess that's correct.

She just nods. "Have you ever had your water tested?"

"No, but doesn't the city have to keep tabs on that?" I think, "Seriously?"

She scribbles on her pad some more. She asks about the trash can, and I point to under the sink.

She opens the baby-safe gear holding the cabinets under the sink together. The trash can is there. She inspects various bottles. Basically there's dish washing soap and dishwasher soap. "Do you have a fire extinguisher?"

I open the pantry and show her the extinguisher. She inspects the date and makes a note. "Is that the only one?"

"No, I have one in the hall by the bedrooms, where the washer and dryer are."

We move to the main area and the sliding door. She opens and closes the door and sees the locking device at the top, which she employs and then confirms that the door does not open.

The coffee table has corner guards on it and is wiped clean. She asks if I have any reclining chairs.

I state that I do not.

She goes back to the entrance and notes the locks on that door and the fire escape route that I have posted. She tells me it looks as though I have done a thorough job and asks if I will show her the bedrooms.

Periodically she types or jots things down as we walk. "Do you live alone?"

"Yes."

"How long have you lived here?"

"Oh, eight, maybe nine years," I reply.

"Have you always lived here alone?"

"No, at one time I was married."

"And you planned to have children?"

"Yes."

We get to the first bedroom, which has the crib. "Is this where you plan for the baby to sleep?"

"Yes." It seems pretty evident.

She measures the slats between the bars of the crib and checks that the mattress is appropriate. She slides her hand in between the crib and the mattress. "Is this new?"

"Yes." I want to say, "I just bought it yesterday," but I don't.

She now focuses on me. "I know you tried to have children. Are you still grieving over the fact that you have been unable to have children?"

I pause and say carefully, "I am not grieving."

"I know you lost a few pregnancies. How did you get over them?"

"I...I...lost, uh, yes, I did lose a few pregnancies, and that is a sad part of my life. They were a while ago, now. And they are sad...sad...memories." I'd like to inform her that you *never get over them*, regardless of going through the five stages of grief that is part of our shared training.

"I see that you are divorced. Do you think that your infertility had anything to do with that?"

Did my infertility have anything to do with our divorce? Probably everything; it certainly started the division. "I think it played a part." I am really glad that my lawyer warned me about her, but really, his questions were quite tame in comparison.

"Are you in contact with your ex-husband? Do you think a baby will bring him back?"

"I am not in contact with my ex-husband." I brace myself for more questions.

"Uh-huh, I see." She types a bit more. "Why aren't you still in contact? Was it a bad divorce?"

Crap! Was it a bad divorce? I control myself and answer only the question. "I guess we split and he moved away and we just have lost contact."

"How did you cope with the divorce?"

A little alcohol, solitude, and drowning myself in my work—that's what comes to mind first. A little alcohol is an honest statement. I don't drink that much; I work far too many hours, and drinking alone is really depressing. "I guess time helps. I get support at work. And I exercise." Support at work is a nice way to say that I hide there.

She nods in her assertive nature. She tests the windows and notes the curtains. There are no pull cords. She looks in the closet, which is mostly empty. She notes the doors with the plastic knob covers to keep them from locking. I put them on both sides of every inside door. I bought twelve and used eleven. She goes into the bathroom that is shared between two of the bedrooms. She checks all of the faucets, the toilet and runs the bath water on hot. "Do you have a bath thermometer?"

"No, do I need one?" I hope I should not have one. It wasn't on the list.

"Do you know what the hot water temperature is set at?"

"One hundred and twenty."

"Isn't that a bit hot? Do you think I could see the water heater?"

"Sure, right now?"

"No, let me see the other bedrooms first."

The second bedroom has a full-size bed. She checks the windows, door, and closet.

"Do you own any firearms?"

"No."

"Any weapons?"

"No." None other than kitchen knives, but I do not want to give her any ideas or any reason to backtrack to the kitchen.

She looks at the backyard, which has a small patio with a few resin chairs and a table. "I see there's no pool."

I nod. "That's right."

We then proceed to the master bedroom, which has a queen bed. She asks, "Are you dating?"

No, not in forever! "Currently I am not dating."

"Do you intend to date?"

"I don't have any intentions." Maybe I should have worded that differently.

"But, say if someone comes into your life, would you date, and would this person stay over or stay for extended periods of time?"

I have no idea. I know my lawyer warned me, but I feel like he should be present. Are these questions fair or legal? It feels like discrimination, but against whom? Single women who don't date? Divorced women with depressing lives and infertility? "Um...I..." I haven't dated since the divorce, but then I don't know, does that make me sound antisocial? "Can I just say that I don't really date, and I have no prospects right now?"

"Sure. But if you did date, could you see another person moving in with you?" She looks directly at me.

She is a persistent bitch; she would probably make a good trial attorney. "I would have to know him very well first and..." I am about to say something negative about marriage, but I notice the wedding ring on the social worker's hand. I am glad I catch myself.

"And?" she prods on.

"And...I have no prospects. Um, I am very cautious." Isn't that what I told my brother to say? Cautious sounds pretty good.

"Cautious, huh? Then why the rush to adopt a baby?" She takes a breath. "Let's start with: why do you want to adopt a child?"

To start with? Oh, shit, how much more of this can I take? I take a deep breath. "I have always wanted to be a parent, and I would love a child to... love."

"Why the rush? Why this child?" Her eyes are rather piercing.

I remember my lawyer asking me the same question, but I can't remember what I said to him. I want to say, why not this child? I can't think of anything. "I feel I was there, and I want this baby." I'm sounding stupid.

"You were there?"

"I helped deliver the baby, and I watched her mom die. And I felt like I was..." I want to say, "there for a reason," but I don't want her to think I am some superstitious idiot. "Um, I...feel like..."

"That's sort of depressing, don't you think? Are you drawn to depressing situations?"

Dumbfounded, I try to make out exactly what she just asked. "I am drawn to the baby. I want to be her mom." I make my point, finally.

"Do you think that you're drawn to the baby as a doctor? The healthcare person who wants to help and be a Good Samaritan?"

"No, I want to be her mom and take care of her." I start to think she resembles a rat, a rather insightful and disturbing rat.

"Do you think you're settling on this child?"

"Settling?" I reply. Maybe I'm just buying a little time to think, but what exactly is she saying?

"Well, this baby may have some disabilities. You know, you are a single mom and a little older...?"

"I want to be her mom." KISS Yup, that's my new motto, rat-face.

"Do you think because you are a doctor that if she has a lifelong illness that you are better equipped to handle it?"

"That might be so." This seems to verify her knowledge of the HIV status.

"But, what if you can't handle it?"

"Pardon me?" I'll kill her with kindness if I have to, the bitch.

"What if her illness cuts into your work or your life, or what if it's not what you think it will be?"

"Well, I think I am better able to understand illnesses than other parents, and I will handle it and cope just like other parents." I hope. Is life ever what anyone expects?

"Do you have any illnesses?"

"No, and I think you have my recent physical, right?"

She nods. "Are you on any prescription medicines?"

"No."

"Do you smoke?"

"No."

"I can't say I pick up any such odors in your home." She says wrinkling her rat nose. "Do you drink?"

"On occasion."

"How many drinks do you have in a week?"

"Two to three, and I don't do any drugs, none, never." I know where she's going next.

"I didn't see any alcohol; do you keep it somewhere hidden?"

"No, I don't keep any. I might pick up a bottle of wine at the store on occasion, but I don't keep bottles."

"May I see your medicine cabinet?"

I point to a door in my bathroom. She inspects bottles and shampoos. She reemerges. "Do you have any criminal record?"

"No. Don't you have all of that information?" I so much want to ask how much longer this will take.

"Yes, but I find it helps to ask." She types a bit and then asks if I'll continue to work.

"Of course." Maybe I should not have said it like that.

"Will you take time off to be with the newborn?"

Oh, rat-woman, that almost sounds hopeful. "I will take off, hopefully five or six weeks."

"Then what?"

"Huh?"

"Who will watch the baby while you are at work?"

"I will need to look into that, but I sometimes work long—no...late hours, so I will probably need to hire a live-in."

"Let's say the baby has a communicable disease. How easy do you think it will be to find someone to live in?"

Fuck, there's a zinger! "I don't know. I guess I'll need to work on that as soon as possible."

"Maybe this will be a bit tougher than you thought? Huh? Maybe you're not really ready for this after all?" She says this a bit triumphantly.

"I am not dissuaded." I wonder if my lawyer's network might be of some help. "Have you helped other parents in such situations?" Helped comes out a bit strained, as I doubt that she is ever helpful.

"Some have stay-at-home partners or parents to help. Do you have parents nearby?"

Bringing my parents into the situation—I am not sure if I'll ever be ready for that. "I do."

"Well, what do they think?" She now starts turning on faucets and inspecting trash cans again.

Shit, I wish I could say, "They'd be delighted, and they support me one hundred percent," but that would be a hoax. "I did not want to tell them until I am more certain." Then I add, "But it is possible." I don't say what is possible. It is possible they will tell me I'm crazy.

She types a bit more. "Health insurance? I figure you have health insurance and adding a child will not be difficult?"

"I suppose."

"What if her medical expenses are really high?"

When will this end? "I have saved up some money because I really don't have many expenses."

"But what if this child eats up all of that? What if you decide you can't handle this? What will you do?"

This is draining. "All I can say is that I think I can handle this, and I think I understand what I am getting into, and I still want to be her mom."

She finishes with the laundry area, the water heater, the fire alarms, the garage, and the backyard. As she finally leaves, she says she will be in touch with my lawyer. I thank her and smile graciously, which is actually hard to do, and say good-bye.

After she finally leaves, I feel exhausted. Some people, you can read when you have won them over, or you get a feel that they are on your side, but with that rat-faced social worker, I really can't say. I'm glad my lawyer gave me a warning call about her! I know I cursed a bit at her in my mind, but I don't think it was evident.

I want to call my lawyer or maybe my brother or my parents. I would call my parents, if I thought they would be supportive. My mom would—no. I can't tell her just yet nor bear to hear her babble right now.

I sit on the sofa and stare straight ahead at nothing.

If I didn't feel so numb, I might get up and mindlessly eat two thousand calories or drink myself silly, but what good would that do? I almost feel like I want to take a long shower and scrub myself clean. Almost, but I can't seem to motivate myself to do anything.

I close my eyes and I rest. I don't sleep. I just rest, and my brain is amazingly quiet.

The next time my lawyer calls, he says he has mixed news. He says it's very likely that we won't have everything in order for me to take the baby home from the hospital. He estimates that we have about two weeks, maybe three weeks at best. He thinks that the baby will be a fost-adopt, but there's no certain plan yet. The first step will be to find foster placement for the infant, and the good news is that the social worker from the hospital says it is not so easy.

The realization that he has called the hospital social worker gives me an awkward feeling.

He rambles on that she says they will likely need a specialized agency, not just any agency and not just any foster parents. She did tell him that I had visited with her regarding the baby and stated my interest. "I'm proud of you for that. Sometimes that first step is the hardest. I think you made an impression on her. She said you are well thought of as a physician at the hospital. I am wondering if she has not contacted the appropriate state agency because she hopes you will be able to step in and take the baby home without...all of that."

Well thought of? Maybe I have one social worker who likes me. "Wait, I thought she told me she had contacted an adoption agency. No, it was a vague referral that she wasn't sure if 'they' had contacted an adoption agency, and I remember wondering who 'they' were."

"No, she has not, and she reports that no adoption agency has been contacted. Further, she informed me that the guardian has no interest in being the foster parent. The social worker is meeting with the guardian tomorrow, and she asked if you and I might want to attend the meeting. We have the guardian's approval. So, what do you think? We've arranged to meet at the social worker's office at ten a.m. Can you attend?"

"Yes." I am stunned. What else can I say?

"If you said no, I would really have to insist." He chuckles. "Good."

"But her office is rather small and cluttered," I blurt out.

"Yes, she said that it was small, but we will just meet there, and then she was going to see what kind of conference room she could arrange. I am hoping that this gives us a leg up, so to speak. So, I will see you tomorrow, at ten a.m. promptly?"

"Uh, yes of course." His "leg up" comment clouds my thoughts with a vision of him in his short shorts. Stop!

"Great." He seems to be winding down and then interjects. "Oh, by the way, how did the home visit go?"

"Have you heard anything?" I hope I do not sound worried.

"No, I have not, which is probably a good thing." Knowingly, he says, "Did she live up to her expectations?"

"Yes, she gave me quite the interrogation."

He softens a bit. "Anything you couldn't handle or felt you didn't handle well?"

"No, I think I kept my cool. Thank you for the heads-up."

"She's never let me down before. Anyway, I am glad that it went smoothly."

"Smoothly is not exactly the right word." I think aloud, "But I am happy to have it behind me."

"Any problems you need to tell me about?"

"No, just it was uncomfortable, but I managed."

"Well, I will see you tomorrow."

"Okay, I will see you at ten a.m.," I confirm.

The hospital meeting...

I arrive at the hospital, and although I have spent countless hours of over a decade there, I feel a little out of sorts. For one thing, I'm not in my comfy scrubs, but a blouse and slacks with a jacket. I smooth my slacks and enter the building. I am just about at the social worker's office, when I see her a few doors down, motioning me into the board room.

I am not late, but everyone else seems to already be there. At the table, my lawyer is seated in a dark suit and a completely blasé tie. There's another man in a dark suit who stands as I enter the room, and I recognize him as the hospital administrator or CEO. The guardian is standing next to him in a skirt suit. The administrator introduces me to the guardian, and we shake hands. The social worker and I are the last to sit. My lawyer pulls out a chair to motion me to sit next to him. We all sit around a dark-wood, oblong table. The leather chairs are comfortable with high backs and casters. There is coffee and water on a side table, and the administrator asks if anyone would like anything. My lawyer smiles and agrees to water for him and for me.

I am glad for the social norms, as I feel stifled. I wonder why the hospital administrator is here. Does my personal business have to become hospital business?

My lawyer begins by affirming that I am interested in fostering and potentially adopting the baby we are here to discuss. He sums up what steps we have taken and what steps we still need to take. He then asks the guardian outright if she has any interest in fostering the child or adopting the child.

"No, I often legally represent children and offer a bridge, so to speak, to help children get into a foster family, or I often help older children, or rather, young adults. I also have children of my own, and so I am happy to try to find another safe home environment for this baby."

The social worker pipes in, "We thought it might be good to meet to find out how we can work together in a confidential manner."

"Yes, confidentiality is paramount, of course," the administrator asserts.

The social worker gives him a nod and continues, "We wanted to be certain of your intentions and see if we could help with paperwork, applications, and so forth so we can discuss this potential placement with you and your lawyer." She gives me a smile.

I notice the administrator nod as well, and I sense support. This is rather unexpected, especially after the social worker made me feel like I didn't have any chance of taking this baby home. Didn't she say something like, just because I was at the delivery, that didn't put me at the front of any list?

The guardian states, "The social worker has told me a bit about you, and I am interested in seeing if you might be a good fit for this child. Certain cases have circumstances that make it harder to find interested parents." She pauses and looks directly at me. "If you are, in fact, interested in this baby, then the social worker and I feel it may be best to try to streamline your application and placement."

Although she is beating around the bush and trying to be confidential, I think we are all well aware that the circumstance is HIV. I also feel that everyone in the room is aware that I am aware of this circumstance and still very interested in this baby. I am probably supposed to say something, but I am starting to feel emotional. I smile and muster, "Thank you," and then with more control, I affirm, "I would like to foster or adopt this baby more than anything."

My lawyer pats my hand and begins to talk with the guardian. For a while, it is as though they are speaking in solitude and the rest of us are just observers. They talk about the application process. He confirms I have had a home visit, and we are waiting on the feedback from that. He will need to set me up for parental training.

I listen intently to them, and I am glad I bought a few books on adoption so I can follow most of what they are saying. During the conversation, the guardian asks about a physical exam and any possible psychological exams. She says it too knowingly.

My mouth is quite dry, and I take a sip of water. Do they all know everything about me, my infertility, and my twin delivery? I did deliver them at this hospital. I must have been deluded to think that everyone didn't know. I mentally shielded myself from that possibility. The hospital is a community all to itself. I never thought of the hospital as my community, and I never realized that it extended all the way to the head administrator. I feel a little queasy and sweaty. But true to my nature, I hide my feelings and concentrate on breathing. I count slowly in my head, willing my heartbeat to a slower pulse.

My lawyer states that everything is in order, and he assures them all that that I am physically and mentally fit. He has looked over all of the documents, and nothing would state otherwise.

I am glad that he sounds so confident. I am also glad that he looks so reassuring, and so...so commonplace.

They start talking about a time table. Once we have completed these tasks, then we can meet and speak more openly. From there, it is probably only a matter of days.

My lawyer asks, "Who is the judge?" The guardian gives him a name, to which he responds, "Oh, yes, I've worked with him before. He's very reasonable." He nods understandingly. They then question when the baby could be expected to leave the hospital.

The administrator announces that the baby could be discharged in anywhere from one to three weeks. But the feeding is going a bit slow, so he is thinking maybe more like three weeks. He gives me a wink.

I smile back and I decide, if nothing else, I need to look and be certain. "Thank you, thank you all. This is very important to me, and I am glad for whatever assistance you have to offer." Well, if it takes the hospital administrator to get this done, then he has my backing. I never really suspected that he was interested in anything but the bottom line of the hospital, my mistake.

We wrap up the meeting, and we exchange handshakes. My lawyer also exchanges cards. He pushes on the back of my elbow and escorts me from the room and out of the hospital.

In the parking lot, he says, "Well, I've never had an experience quite like this one, and I don't like to get too hopeful, but I think you are very close to motherhood." He sings the word motherhood. I note that the pitch of his voice is a little higher and his gesticulations return once we are out of earshot of the hospital. He smiles and says he will call me later this afternoon. We have more items to discuss. Before parting, he cheers with a bursting expression, two fists and a little cha-cha dance move.

I am very happy. I get into my car, and I have a funny feeling that the hospital community is watching me. I realize they have been there all along, and I am fine with that.

More follow-up phone calls...

My lawyer calls, and he immediately jumps in. "I have never had a case where the potential parent has met the baby and made intentions known to the hospital and powers that be, before meeting with a lawyer or agency, but I must say, it has its benefits. It also doesn't hurt that everyone in the hospital knows and likes you. It's funny because I wouldn't have said that I warmed right up to you. Maybe it's just that they have known you all of these years."

I am silent.

"Oh, don't take that the wrong way. You came so highly recommended by your brother and even when I talked to the hospital social worker. But you just come across so serious, and somewhat like a wounded bird."

He's so giddy that I wonder if he's had a drink or two, or if he always prattles with such honesty. I recall our first meeting and know that the answer is the latter.

He continues, "Well, as I said, I think that went really well. I think that since you had told the social worker your intentions, she probably voiced them to the guardian, and then I called at the right time. I presume that together they thought it might be easier for all parties involved to go with the lady-doctor, or you who show great interest in the adoption of the child, rather than getting specialized agencies involved and taking a chance on finding another parent match. I am sure that I do not have to tell you, but the circumstance that might make it hard to find interested parents is..." He waits for me to finish his sentence.

"HIV," I reply.

"Yes, I believe you are right. So, it is good that you are interested, but there is one thing that might stand in your way of permanently parenting this child. Do you know what that is?"

"Um."

Before I can answer, he says, "It would be if a family member surfaced, either now or during your foster period. I know what you are wondering."

It's good that he does, because I am not sure what to think; I'm up and I'm down.

"You're wondering if once the child is officially adopted by you, if someone from the child's family can surface and take the baby away from you. And the answer is, no, not in this state. So you can take one of two paths here. You can just foster the child and wait whatever the designated time period is to adopt, or you could look into a private investigator, even now, to get a better perspective."

"I have been doing some reading, and I am wondering if the state has an obligation to look for someone? Isn't that what the foster time period is for?" I think I sound knowledgeable.

"Oh, sure, the state, meaning the social workers involved or an agency, if there were one, who might attempt to look for someone. But trust me; they have other things to do. Also, they don't really suffer if a family member comes forward. Their main job is to place the child in a safe and hopefully loving environment. The only person who will suffer if a family member comes forward is you, and likely the child. The thought on the foster time period is that if there is a concerned family member, it would give that person time to come forward. I guess in this case, maybe word of the funeral to a long-lost boyfriend who finds out she died shortly after giving birth, and puts two and two together, and wonders if he's the father, and then starts asking about the baby's whereabouts."

"Well, what do you recommend?"

"In your case, and actually in all cases, I would recommend getting a private investigator, at least to do a fair amount of digging. I think that once you become attached to having the baby in your home, you will sleep better at night."

"Okay, so how do I go about finding a good private investigator?" This is rhetorical, as I know he has a connection.

"Well, I happen to know a guy who's helped me before, and I hope that you are not upset with me to know that I have already contacted him and gave him some generalized bits of your story, and I got a quote for you." And he gives me the quote for about two weeks of working on the case. He breaks it down into the hourly rate and the proposed number of hours.

"What did you tell him?" I am not really upset, because I know he has to keep things moving, but I just want some information.

"Oh, don't worry; your secrets are safe! I just told him I have a client who wishes to adopt a baby and knows about some of the maternal side of the baby, but nothing about the paternal side. Then I asked him about how long it would take him to find out such information. When he said about two weeks, I asked him if he would be available for the next two weeks, and could he give me a quote so I could propose it to my client. "

I am fairly certain I have no more secrets. I have been completely revealed, and it wouldn't surprise me if my adoption file with my psychological evaluation isn't somewhere locatable on the web. "I am not really all that worried about my secrets anymore. I felt pretty exposed today in the meeting, and I am all right with it. I think I was the only one who didn't realize that everyone at the hospital knew my business—the infertility, the twins, the divorce. I realize they were there through it all. And I am good with all of it."

"You're correct, and I think that's part of why they are all cheering for you." He gets back to the question. "So what do you think about the PI?"

I think over the quote for a second or two, and I surmise that given how quickly everything is going, I probably will not spend as much as some of the books have quoted; and as I did say to the home inspector, I do have some money saved up. "Sure, do you want to give me his number?"

"I have his number right here," he says and rattles off the name and number. "If you don't mind, I'll call him and get the ball rolling. I will have to send him the information I have about the mother, and then I probably have to call and get permission from the current guardian."

"So should I just wait to hear from him?"

"Yes, that would probably be best."

"Should we wait until we are more certain about placement?"

"That's up to you, but I was thinking that he could be done by the time you take your baby home. So do you want me to go ahead and call him?"

"Yes." I yield. "I like how efficient everything has been so far."

"Yes, me too," he agrees. "I also have another thought, which is a bit unorthodox." He continues, "The hospital social worker spoke with the patient's stepmom, and I was wondering if you would want to try to talk with the stepmom. You could ask her directly about the family history and find out if there are any other relatives or friends or boyfriends."

I stiffen. "Is this something I should do?"

"Well, maybe when the time is right."

"I am not sure I am following what you are saying."

"I am just saying that either you or the PI will need to ask a little more about the—" And then he pauses a second. "You, of course, understand the terms MOB and FOB, right?"

"Of course." Mother of baby and father of baby instantly register.

"Well, in this case, I think it would be easy for you to investigate the MOB's side of the family, and you might want to know them better."

Know them better—I am still not following him well at all. "But the stepmom wants nothing to do with the baby; well, that's what I was led to believe. Why would I want to know her or them better?"

"First of all, it is easy to get in contact with her now. Second, although you may want nothing to do with her or them, your baby, assuming all goes well, will probably want to know them. I may be jumping a bit forward, and maybe you want to wait until you are really going to care for the baby, but it's just a simple meeting. Tell her you want to get information for when your baby starts asking questions. Maybe even ask if she might want you to send her updates or photos. It sounds like the baby will have an aunt or half aunt."

I am silent, but all of this is registering in my brain. I had only been thinking of myself and my family, but in reality, there is another known family. My book reading has told me that adopted kids often question and search for their biological families. "I am catching on. Do you recommend I try to get her number, and can I openly ask for it?"

"I said, at the right time. I feel I need to prepare you, because things may happen rather fast. Also, people move around a lot these days, so I am thinking you should make some contact while you know her whereabouts. On another note, do you know if the patient's funeral has taken place or what arrangements have been made?"

My lawyer seems to be quite the PI himself. "No, honestly, I haven't given that much thought." I instantly feel that I have been quite self-absorbed.

"I'll talk to the PI soon and get back to you with those details. I know he will want to attend, if it hasn't taken place already, and maybe you should as well."

"Okay." I realize my journal will be very important to document the burial. Should I take photos?

He interrupts my thoughts. "I will call the PI, and either he or I will call you back. What's next on my list? Ah, yes. What are you doing the next two days?"

"I have nothing tomorrow, but the next day I am at the hospital for twenty-four hours."

"How do you do that? Don't you get tired?"

"I don't do it too often. It's a double shift, because I had to change a shift for the home inspection."

"I signed you up for a course, the home training course, or parental training course. It's tomorrow and it goes two days." He gives me more specifics.

It's in a hotel along the interstate, located between two larger cities, our city and another, that way they combine more prospective parents. He has me set up for the conference, and he gives me the hotel number so I can call and arrange a room. I will need to bring a checkbook and pay at the course in the morning. The day starts at 8:00 a.m. with check-in. The classes go from about 8:30 a.m. until 3:30 p.m. on both days. "You can eat at the hotel; there's not much choice," he says lightly. "There will be many people wanting to adopt children, mostly couples. I wouldn't tell them that you are trying to adopt a child in only two to three weeks. That might set some people off, if you know what I mean?" he warns, and yet he encourages me to circulate his name.

"But what if I miss the funeral?"

"I think we have to put everything into perspective, and this course is something you need to do in order to complete your application process. You should feel pretty lucky to have one occur with such opportune timing."

"All right." What more can I say?

"Bring your checkbook. I don't think they will take a credit card the day of the course, and expect a late fee too."

"Bring my checkbook. I've got it." I simply have to do what I have to do.

"So, don't worry about the PI; I'll get him going. You just concentrate on your course."

First I look up the location of the hotel and get general directions, which are easy: leave town, stay on the interstate about eighty miles. I call and arrange a room. I call to change my earlier shift, so now I'll get back into town and work twenty-four hours starting in the evening, rather than in the morning. Personally, I would rather have the last twelve hours be at night, but I am glad the change was easy. I start to pack an overnight bag. I was glad to see on the web that they have a pool and fitness room, which will give me something to do in the evening. I'm pulling some outfits when the phone rings.

I answer and it's the PI my lawyer told me about. He has a deep, raspy voice, and I already pin him as a smoker, or a prior smoker. He has gotten some papers by fax already from the lawyer. He asks me some more specifics about the job. Then he gets to the real reason that he called, his fee. He goes over the same numbers I heard from my lawyer, and then he asks for half up front and he would be happy to take a credit card over the phone.

Of course he would. No time to back down, so I give him the number.

"I understand that you will be in a course for two days and that I should not contact you by phone. But I would like to give you some updates, and I might have some questions. Is it okay if I text or e-mail?"

"Yes, you can do either." I confirm my cell number and e-mail address.

He says it's been a pleasure.

The home training course...

I awake at 5:00 a.m. I quickly make coffee and get dressed, and I am on the road with my overnight bag. Once I leave the city and its suburbs, there's not much but open road.

I arrive before 7:30 a.m. Of course, my room is not ready because they are just teeming with business. The hotel is out on its own. There was a small town about fifteen miles prior to reaching my destination, so if I need to get away or if the food is horrible, I can venture out.

I wait in the lobby, reading one of my books. The book is on adoption, which I decoy within a magazine. I note several other guests arriving and getting situated in their rooms. I know I only called for a room last night, but I did call ahead.

At 8:00 a.m., I tuck my adoption book-magazine into my oversized purse, and I find the conference room and sign in. I write a check; no, they do not take credit cards. There is a substantial late fee, showing that desperate people will pay! In return, they hand me a packet and ask me to fill out a name badge and list my city.

The lady at the desk looks chatty. "If you're anxious enough to get in and pay the late fee, you must be close to your adoption?" She smiles contagiously.

I smile back, but not quite as radiantly. My mouth parches and my stomach churns. I swallow with some difficulty, and then I hesitantly tell her, "I may be close, but it's not certain yet." I hope she doesn't ask any more questions. The late fee was, well, almost double the cost, but it's nothing compared to the PI and legal fees I'm sure to accrue.

Her smile fades a bit. "Oh...Well, best of luck."

"Thanks," I say as I turn to find a seat.

"Don't let them string you along. If you need help or advice, let me know," she adds watchfully.

I turn slowly around. "Thank you, I'll keep that in mind." I luck out, as a couple is approaching the table, and she goes on to flash her pearly whites at them.

The room has long tables and chairs, high school grade, facing a screen, a typical set-up. On one wall there is a table with juice, coffee, and pastries.

I find a seat near the back, and I am glad to see water pitchers and cups on each row of tables. I venture to the modest buffet. I grab juice and more coffee and a pastry, a cheese Danish in a warmed cellophane wrapper. I don't think I've had this kind of breakfast pastry in years. The Danish is just as I recall, somehow reminiscent of something I can't quite put my finger on, maybe road trips as a kid and spending the night at just such a roadside hotel.

More people file in, mostly couples, but a few singles like myself. I wonder what brings us all here; adoption, of course, but all of us have stories. A female couple sits at my table. There's a guy who appears to have brought his mom, but I would never assume that. Although I wonder about other people's stories, I adamantly hope that we do not play the game where we each have to verbally share what brought us here.

We are eighteen in total. At the front of the class, there is a table of four speakers. They introduce themselves as a couple who recently adopted a child, a social worker, and a child developmental specialist.

They go over the syllabus. This morning, it shows that we will talk about child development, and this will be run by the developmental specialist, my chatty friend from the welcome table. Some subtopics read: Child Health, Developmental Milestones, Picking a Pediatrician, Immunizations, Health Issues and International Adoption...and so on. This afternoon will be devoted to child safety and will be run by the social worker and the developmental specialist. I note there is some lettering after the child developmental special-ist's name, but I am not sure what it denotes. There's no N, so I don't think she is a nurse, and I don't think she's a social worker or PhD. Maybe it's a teaching degree, oh well. Then the couple, "Who have so graciously volunteered their time," will tell their story. Finally, there will be some small group sessions.

By lunch, my buttocks are already tired of sitting, and I need to walk around a bit. I do not believe I have learned anything, and things that I did learn, mostly about foreign adoption, do not pertain to me. The ladies at my table ask me if I want to join them for lunch. I really want to say no, but I do not want to be rude. I ask them if they are going directly to the café, although truck stop or diner might be a better description. They tell me they are, and I tell them that I have yet to check in and I am not certain how long the process will take. I thank them and agree that they should go ahead without me. I stretch as I say this, and I tell them I might also need to walk around a bit, but maybe I can I join them later, if they are still eating? They say certainly.

I leave most of my items at the desk except for my purse. I need some air, and so I head outside. As I walk around the parking lot and the small pool, I try to come up with what lie to tell these ladies. If I tell them I am an obstetrician/gynecologist, I will have to answer innumerable questions about their health, fertility, or infertility. Once I was at a party and a woman told me all about her breast mass and she wanted me to examine it right then in a back room. No, I am not an OB today! I am not examining anything, any breast, knee, abscess, nodule, or scar. I try to come up with something that they will ask very few questions about. Today, I am a receptionist at a medical building.

There's very little area to walk, unless I want to walk around the cars in the parking lot. Somehow, I think I would look lost or that I am staking out other peoples' cars. Rather than looking lost or like a thief or walking in small circles; I get my bag from my car and then reenter the hotel.

I check into my room, which is now ready. The room is typical: two full-sized beds, each with an oak backboard and a side lamp; one picture of an outdoor scene; a matching oak dresser with a TV on one end; drab curtains; and an air conditioning unit by the window. I put my bag on the empty end of the dresser and immediately start stretching. I instinctively roll my shoulders, not that the bag was heavy. I roll my head side to side. I stretch my hands up to the ceiling and arch my back.

How did I ever sit through hours and hours of daily lectures in college and medical school? Then from lectures I would study for countless hours at desks in the library or in any quiet location. I shake my head at the thought. I guess I was used to sitting then.

I continue to stretch and bend at the waist. I note the carpet's signs of wear. The comforters are not too shabby. Then I notice two black spots on the comforter. One is a bit of fuzz, but the other is harder to discern...

"Oh, no! No, don't think about it!" I try to command my mind. "Bed bug epidemic." Okay, I thought about it, and there's no going back. Sometimes, I wish I could have the bliss of ignorance. I wish I didn't always have to think so much, but that is not me. I further inspect the speck; it's not moving. I don't think it's a tiny insect, not alive at least. I bend down and lift the comforter. Going around the bed, I expose the mattress. I inspect the seams because I think I read to do that somewhere. I stretch as I make my way around each of the beds as if I am not really looking for bugs. I do not see any, but regardless of what I find, I will be itching for days.

I give in and fully investigate. I convince myself that I do not see any moving bugs and that I do not need to speak to management about changing rooms, or rather sleep in my car, or perhaps make the drive back home for the night. I tidy one of the beds while taking mental notes. I think of a shopping list: trash bags, Lysol, rubbing alcohol, and Benadryl. This evening I will have to visit that small town to do some shopping. I stand up, and I am a little lightheaded. I wish I had brought a few beverages from home for the room. I add some groceries to the list too.

By the time I get to the diner, the ladies who invited me to lunch are leaving. I see them exiting through a different door, and so I don't bother to try to get their attention. They are parting from a group of five, and I assume they lunched with a few others from the class. I realize I am a little antisocial, to which I am ambivalent. On the one hand, all of these people could become a great support group. We could hold gatherings and share references/resources. We could even get together once we adopt kids and see how they are all growing—maybe even post photos on a group website. On the other hand, none of that appeals to me. As a physician, I have been taught to closely observe others, to gather information about their case, and to come up with a diagnosis and regimen. I have been informed to have empathy, not sympathy, and not to become too closely involved with patients. Possibly this mantra has permeated more than just my professional career. I sit by myself and order a chicken sandwich. I wonder if I am late to the afternoon class if they will take off points. The class is too small to get away with being late.

The afternoon class is about safety, from car seats to SIDS and even basic baby and child CPR. We break into small groups to practice CPR on baby and child dummies. This goes a bit into overtime. Luckily, once we feel we have mastered the techniques, we are free to go. It's not hard to tell the ones who have done this before; we are the first to leave. Actually, a few of us leave, and a few stay to help and give pointers to the others. I am glad to be getting out before anyone asks me what I do. Thankfully, I didn't get the chance to lie to the ladies at lunch about my job, because if they ask me in class, I will have to tell the truth. As we are leaving, the social worker announces that we will hear the adoption story tomorrow, and we will start promptly at 8:00 a.m. He asks that we arrive a little before eight. He also states that if anyone wants to get together tonight for some group therapy and discussions, meet him in the lobby at 7:45 p.m.

I make a mental note to steer clear of the lobby at 7:45 p.m.

I hope that we get out on time tomorrow, because I have to head back into town to work at the hospital.

I return to my room, and I am about to call the co-worker I switched calls with to warn her in case I am a little late. My phone shows three texts have come through from the PI.

The first is from about 10:30 a.m.:

"The patient had an autopsy, and her stepmom had her cremated. Not sure where remains are or if any funeral services are arranged."

The next is about 1:00 p.m.:

"It looks like I will need to contact the stepmom to see if there is a funeral. I heard you may want to speak to her also, but I will make contact."

The last is about 3:20 p.m.:

"I have two messages to the stepmom, but no response. I have the name of MOB's commuter college; I plan to snoop around there tomorrow. Call if you have any questions."

I am not sure if I need to call, so I just text back at 4:20 p.m.:

"Out of class now. Call me if you think we need to talk. Otherwise, your texts are informative. Thanks."

I decide to search on my phone about the nearby town to see what's there. It would be great if there is a park to go walk and get some fresh air. There's not much on the Internet, so I call the welcome center number, and they give me directions to a park. I recognize the name of the town from a few of my patients. Just the name makes me think of a few women and their obstetrical issues. Now, I can assimilate where they come from.

I can't get there fast enough. I would like to leave my phone, but you never know when you might need assistance. I find the park, which is picturesque small-town. It's near a high school, and there's a running path that meanders around ball fields and playgrounds where there are some moms pushing their children on swings. Perfect; I walk for about forty minutes. I wonder what it would be like to live here. I wonder what it is like to bring your child to a park and push the child on a swing. Everyone looks so happy. There's a peaceful and somewhat idyllic feeling to the town. I try to envision myself living here, but it just doesn't feel right.

The town is not hard to navigate, and I find a small grocery store, where I buy large trash bags. As soon as I leave the hotel room, I will place my duffle bag in a trash bag and tie it in a knot. I buy Lysol to spray in the trash bag to make it less hospitable for any bugs and keep the contents smelling fresh. I buy rubbing alcohol to swab exposed areas of my car. When I get to the hospital, I will get some clean scrubs, place my worn clothes in another trash bag, and take a hot shower and change.

Is this overkill? Maybe, but I had lice once, and these small measures now are nothing compared to those needed to get rid of such nasty pestilence. I can precisely recall the horrid feeling of finding lice on my scalp. I washed my hair with anti-nit shampoo several times, each time having to pass a thinly spaced comb along my scalp while trying to get rid of the nits. This gave me a new appreciation of the terms, "going over with a fine-toothed comb," and "nit-picking." I bought anti-lice hair spray to discourage any further infestations. I did loads of laundry, I tossed out pillows and hair brushes, and I bagged up bedding for weeks. I had to tell my co-workers and the hospital, which steam cleaned every inch of our sleep rooms. No one else seemed to have them, but they had to have come from the hospital. I can't figure out where else they would have come from. My hairdresser said they're crafty. She told me about the dangers of head rests, sharing helmets and/or hats. She told me to be wary of trying on any hair accessory or hat in a store. I probably didn't need her to add to my phobia.

Call me neurotic, but an ounce of prevention will help me sleep at night— that and Benadryl.

The grocery store has a small deli section, and the worker at the counter makes me a nice sandwich. At check out, I have plastic trash bags, Benadryl, rubbing alcohol, Lysol, a six-pack Styrofoam cooler, a few sodas, a pint of milk, a small bag of frozen peas to keep items cold, chips, a bag of bagels, and cream cheese. I ask the cashier for a dinner recommendation, and he gives the name of a good barbecue restaurant, just a little south on the feeder.

The barbecue is savory, and I overeat. It's about 7:00 p.m., and I better get back to the hotel if I want to miss the therapy session, and I do.

I settle into my room for the night. I toss the semi-frozen peas out and get some ice from the maker down the hall. I pull the comforter and blanket off of one of the beds and place them on a chair. I inspect the bed again, but I don't notice anything. What would I do if I did see a bed bug? Would I really sleep in the car? I raise the thermostat a touch, as I will just be sleeping under the sheet. I take a Benadryl with some water. I take a shower and watch some TV before sleeping. I sleep well, and for some reason I don't feel so apprehensive. I am also glad to be going to the hospital tomorrow, and I can't wait to check on the baby girl. The word *daughter* comes to mind and makes me smile, but I know I'm not quite there yet.

The next morning I rise early and have a bagel and hotel room brewed coffee. I could wait and just get coffee at the conference, but at least I now have real milk to put in my coffee and not that powdered "whitener." I wish I could toast the bagel, but the cream cheese makes it palatable. Ah, here's why I couldn't move to a small town. I can buy a regular bagel with cream cheese, but can I get a cheddar bagel with jalapeños topped with guacamole and sprouts?

I check to see if there is a newspaper at my door, and there is not. Instead there is a note reporting that if you're here for the parenting course, not to worry about check out. The hotel will delay check out until the course ends. Well, that is good news. I turn on a TV news station while I get ready for the day.

I try to arrive at the small conference room as close to 8:00 a.m. as possible. The volunteer couple has already begun their story. I sign in, and the child developmental specialist is just as cheerful as yesterday. "Oh, ma'am, you did not tell us where to send your transcript. Do you want us to send it to this address?" She is pointing to an address that is not mine.

At first I am a little worried and I check that she has the right person. My address is at the top, under my name, but for correspondence… "Ah, that's my lawyer's address. Is that customary to send the transcript to the lawyer or agency?"

"Well, they will certainly want a copy for your file."

"Can I have a copy?" I say, but I am certain I already know the answer.

"Of course you can, but there is an extra fee."

"Which is...?" I inquire expectantly.

She pulls out a chart, for one transcript, two transcripts, three, and so forth. The first is included in the course fee, and the second and such are further divided into the copying fee, authorization fee, and mailing fee.

Nickel and dime. "Do I have to decide this right now?"

"Try to let me know today. If you have to call it in later, there are other fees, for locating the transcript and a requisition form and fee. It's a little much, I know."

I'm sure she doesn't know.

The social worker has returned to the desk, and, listening in, he says, "Oh, it's not that bad anymore. You can request it online nowadays. If you look in your course work, the website is listed somewhere. It might be a little more money, but it's not much."

"All right, I'll see if I ever need another one in the future and then request it." I glance over at the screen to show interest.

The social worker says, "Yeah, get in there; it's a good story!"

As human nature dictates, I and almost every other person sit in the same seat as yesterday. I set my stuff down, and then I go to get more coffee as quietly as I can. I have had so much hospital coffee over the years that I am not too picky, but I don't bother with the coffee "whitener."

It seems I only missed the couple's introductions, their names, and jobs. The couple adopted a daughter from China. They had infertility problems. The lady rolls her eyes. "I'm sure none of you knows anything about that, huh?" They did a lot of research over the Internet and found some reputable agencies that dealt with such adoptions. They did get resources. The lady grins. "Actually, we had the best resource—my sister; she also adopted a baby from China."

I miss a fraction of their story as I hear that this woman and her sister are likely both infertile, and I try to figure out what genetic disorder might affect two sister siblings, some sort of mosaicism, Turner's perhaps—or endocrine related, such as premature ovarian failure...I run through a differential and realize the futility.

The guy adds, "You hear the word transracial, but in our extended family, we don't even think about that."

"We had the best agency, and they only billed us as we went," she says.

"Yes, be wary of agencies that request a lot of money up front," he adds.

"I knew we were on the right track the first time I got to see my baby. Our agency links to another agency in China, and you can Internet chat with your prospective baby; it's so cool!"

Then photos come up of their baby looking directly into the camera, a full head shot with big eyes. They flash lots of photos of visiting their baby and visiting China. The photos are labeled. They show the orphanage. There's a photo of the three of them waving as they are getting on an airplane.

"We heard of horror stories where the baby they showed you on the Internet, or in photos, was no longer available when you got to whichever country you were hoping to adopt from, and so it was a wasted trip, or they did have another baby who was ill in some way and could be adopted immediately. So you could either take that baby or go home empty-handed and in debt," the guy warned.

"We were so excited; really everything went according to plan. There are a lot of steps, from picking out an agency, going to a course like this, home inspection..." she chimes in.

There's an overall groan from the audience following the mention of home inspection.

"Visiting the baby online and then in person, arranging the trip, and visiting foreign government agencies," he continues.

"Yeah, that was a little scary," she affirms.

They're so cute the way they banter back and forth, completing each other's thoughts.

"And then there were government fees to pay and international paperwork and legal fees...and when all that settles, you bring your baby back home, and you repeat those same steps here."

"Yeah."

"Then when you finish all of the paperwork and legal processes, it's time to start the medical workup."

"Make sure, if you adopt internationally, that you get a good recommenda-tion for a pediatrician."

"Ours did a thorough evaluation, even looking through her hair for lice and stool for, uh, worms, I guess."

"And urine and blood."

I comment in my mind that I would hope the pediatrician was thorough and would check for all of that.

"And then she had to catch up with immunizations."

"All in all, we are very happy."

"Very happy, and we hope you all have happy adoptions too!"

"And we might even adopt a second sometime."

The couple exchanges hopeful grins.

They end with trusted websites and resources. They flash their e-mails, which are also in our syllabi in case we want to contact them.

I feel genuinely happy for them.

Ms. Perky comes along and interrupts. "Thank you so much. I think it's won-derful to hear a success story. Let's give them a round of applause of thanks."

We all clap. The couple is beaming.

The social worker comes up and gets us back on track with the syllabus. "First I have an announcement, that the last hour, 'Pitfalls of Foreign Adop-tion' is optional. So if you do not plan to adopt internationally, you could skip that session. If you are not certain, I'd recommend that you stay. Most people stay because, honestly, some of the scenarios can happen even here."

Today's subheadings read: Baby-Proof House, Managing Your Temper and Managing Your Toddler, Respite for Parents/Time Out for Kids, and more. The social worker is entertaining, and he shows lots of funny slides of toddlers covered in spaghetti or writing on the wall with crayons. It's hard not to imagine these scenarios are somewhere in my future. I don't think I could be mad at child graffiti on the wall. I think I might want to frame it.

Before I know it, it's time for lunch. The ladies next to me do not invite me to sit with them again.

I go to my room and have a sandwich, chips, and a soda. I check my messages.

The PI texts at 11:46 a.m.:

"I went to her campus. I met her landlord and work contact at the library. I had a brief talk with the stepmom. On your drive home, call me to discuss."

I lie on the bed for a while, and I am glad for the silence.

Soon it's time to pack my things. I load the duffle bag into a trash bag. I put my stuff into the car with the cooler, with fresh ice, in the front seat on top of an open trash bag. This way, I can get a beverage if I need one, and when I get home, I can just pull up the trash bag and toss the whole thing. I check out of the hotel before the last segment of the conference. I hope to save time from everyone checking out at once, in case I am in a hurry.

I have two more sessions, "Sexuality: Know Your Limits," a summary lecture, and then questions. The lectures go by quickly, but the questions go on and on. Hands are raised to ask questions, and the social worker knows most of the questioners by name. I perceive that many attended the group therapy last night. The social worker finally says, "After I get to all of your questions and we have a small break, we will talk about the pitfalls of foreign adoption. But if you need to be going, the desk will check you out." A handful of us get up and stand in line at the desk to check out, but the majority is desperate to help clarify their situations.

We were given a questionnaire the first day and essentially checking out consists of handing in the questionnaire. Two people have no idea about the questionnaire. The helper at the desk has some available to give them so they can sit back down and fill them out. I turn mine in with my name tag and sign some form verifying my attendance. I avoid any chitchat by simply saying, "Thank you," then turning and heading straight to my car.

I leave the hotel at about 3:30 p.m. I call the PI on the way home, and he updates me with what he knows so far. The patient was a student at a commuter college. She lived in a small apartment. He called the landlord. He really didn't know her but said that she was rarely late in paying her rent. The landlord doesn't live in her building, so he wouldn't know about her friends.

The PI tells me, "I talked with a few nearby tenants to see if they remembered her. Some said they did, but no one knew her more than just a passerby. She did a work-study program, working in the library. The librarian had little to say about her other than she showed up at work and was good at shelving books." The PI sighs and goes on. "The librarian could not say much about her friends or if she had a study group, but commented that she, the patient, had only worked there about three or maybe four months. I still have some digging around on campus to do. I plan to talk with her counselor tomorrow, and then I'll see if any of her professors or classmates might know something about her, but so far I don't have much to go on."

"So no one in the apartment building remembers any boyfriends or anything like that."

"No, no boyfriends," he confirms. "But I still have some digging. I probably haven't gotten anywhere near her inner circle of friends."

"So you'll keep me posted."

"Actually, I am going to meet with the stepmom. I reached her. She, uh…" He stumbles a bit. "She didn't exactly give me a warm fuzzy feeling, if you know what I mean." He gives a raspy chuckle. "But she says she will meet me or us one day while her daughter is at school, probably not tomorrow, but the next day. I will need to get a definite time, and I'll probably need to keep on her so she doesn't back out."

"Oh, I would like to meet her. I mean, I would like to go to the meeting."

"I figured you might, especially since she's the one definite contact we have. So I'll call you tomorrow with those plans, all right?"

"Okay," I respond automatically. Then, I change topics, "Did you see the results of the autopsy?"

"Oh yeah, from what I can tell, she died of a pneumonia. I think the symbol is PCP, which I learned is not a mind-altering substance." He laughs a little gruffly. "Her toxicology screens were all negative. That's basically it. I can fax it to you, or I'll give you a copy when we arrange to meet the stepmom."

"Can you e-mail the report to me? Is that possible?"

"Sure, I can manage that," he affirms.

"Okay, then I'll wait to hear from you next."

"Uh-huh, talk to you soon." With that, he hangs up.

The drive home is quick, just a straight highway, and there's no traffic going into town. The lanes coming out of town look to be just the opposite, bumper to bumper.

At home, I first take all of my bed bug precautions, bagging up the duffle bag and all clothes, tossing out the cooler and food, swabbing my car, and showering. I have time for a work out and another shower before I head in for work. I will have to check how long I need to keep everything bagged up. I laugh at myself, as I know I will probably double that time. Eventually I'll take out the clothes and wash them, but for now, I place them on a shelf in the garage. They are only two small bags on a shelf, but I am glad I have already had my home inspection, because if I hadn't, I would probably throw the bags away rather than having to answer any probing questions.

I make it to work on time, and stop off at the cafeteria for dinner. Let's see, dried-out chicken and overdone canned vegetables or mystery meatloaf and mashed potatoes; I choose the second option. The food lacks imagination, but it's hearty.

I get a happy feeling while I am eating, not from the food, but from an urge to visit the baby. I tend to the few things I have to, and then I head to the NICU.

My badge unlocks the door. There's an anteroom where you have to scrub your hands and don a yellow gown. I am a little timid because I am not certain I should be here, but then, I can't stay away. The neonatologist sees me through the glass and smiles and waves me in. I go through the next door.

"I've heard a rumor that you might be adopting a very special little girl."

I nod and smile back. I figured that might have been why he was smiling.

"Well, that's so nice." He nods enthusiastically. "We are just starting to feed her. Would you like to try?"

My usual inner alarm warns me that I might become attached. And then what if I am not the one to adopt her? But nothing can stop me. I have to try. I have to try. I always try, and I usually fail. I want to try.

It looks as though the nurse is going to feed the baby, but the neonatologist interrupts her and asks her to help me do it. He's so peppy and directed, I wonder if anyone ever tells him no.

I sit next to the warmer, and the nurse hands me the baby. I melt.

Like I was frozen for innumerable years, only to reach this moment and truly melt.

She's bundled in a blanket and a cap so that only her little face sticks out. She has a cute nose that is flattened. She has full and ready lips. Newborns are designed this way to latch on. She eagerly accepts the bottle with a good sucking mechanism for such a tiny baby.

I stay for ten to twenty minutes, but it feels much longer. I have to go back to work, and I say good-bye.

As I work, I'm floating on a cloud.

I check on the baby here and there. I want to seem caring, but I don't want to be a nuisance.

Twenty-four hours later, just after 6:00 p.m., I get home, and I am tired. I got a little rest here and there, but the work was rather steady. I am glad to have had the time I did in the nursery, after which even when I might have slept, I couldn't. I make myself a snack and check my phone.

There is a text from the PI, from 4:00 p.m.:

"I have arranged for us to meet the stepmom tomorrow. Give me a call."

I wonder how I missed that while I was working.

I call the PI.

"Hello, I've been expecting your call," he answers. I am sure his cell phone identified me. "I have arranged for us to meet the stepmom tomorrow at ten thirty a.m. I had hoped to get your okay for the time, but I went ahead and accepted because I didn't want to miss the opportunity, as she has not been that easy to reach." He delves on, "Her daughter is in preschool, or maybe kindergarten, in the mornings. She will allow us an hour to meet with her. Are you free tomorrow for the meeting?"

"Yes, where are we meeting?"

"She wants us to meet at her home. I will e-mail you her address, but I think it would be good for us to meet ahead of time and come up with questions, given that we only have an hour."

"Okay," I agree.

"Let me look at the area of her address on the Internet and find a café where we can meet ahead of time, say nine thirty a.m.," he puts forth. "I will include the meeting place in my e-mail, all right?"

"All right," I agree.

"I'll do this right now, so you should get an e-mail within the next twenty minutes."

We hang up.

I am not sure I can stay awake another twenty minutes to wait for his e-mail. I finish my snack, and then I get ready for bed. I am not sure where I am going tomorrow, so I must stay awake in order to get the e-mail, map out the directions, and plan what time to wake up accordingly.

Reading his e-mail, I calculate the distance and time in my head. I won't need to make breakfast since we are meeting at a café. I allow thirty minutes to get dressed and an extra fifteen minutes, just in case, so 8:00 a.m. I set the alarm and I collapse into bed.

Contact with the stepmom...

Before meeting the stepmom, I meet the PI at a café, and while sipping coffee we go over questions we want to ask her. I also order a gingerbread muffin, which is baked to perfection.

I mainly wish to know about the family history, if there are any other relatives, and whether she wants me to keep in touch. The PI shakes his head almost imperceptibly as I mention keeping in touch. He is curious about college bills and phone records, but he is not certain that she will "even be that helpful."

I follow him in my car, driving to the house.

The neighborhood has few regulations. The sidewalks look to be an afterthought. Some homes have multiple children's toys scattered on the lawns; a few others have truck and machine parts. One home is pink and has a flock of flamingos with windmill-like wings in the foreground. The stepmom's home is a nondescript, white, one-story home with a corrugated aluminum porte cochere.

The stepmom invites us in. The house is musty and full of smoke. There are many ashtrays with various butts and ashes. She explains that her daughter is at school, but she will need to go pick her up in a little bit. She motions for us to sit, but she doesn't offer any refreshments.

There is a small cluster of baby items, and I am hopeful that she was supportive of the baby.

We sit down, and the PI asks many questions about her late husband and if there are any other relatives.

Her husband died about three years ago, "rest his soul." From some kind of cancer, "I can't remember if it was bladder or prostrate."

Prostate, I correct her in my mind.

"After he died, well, I was never very close with my stepdaughter. I think she was a student or something. I didn't really keep tabs on her, you know?" She starts smoking. "I am kind of surprised that I am her next of kin. I really don't feel like I should be. Of course, if there were another next of kin, she would have probably hit them up for money too. I rarely saw her, and I will tell you that lately with the way she would dress, I am pretty certain she was prostituting herself. I don't know if that's how she was getting through school or what she was up to." She gives a slanted smile.

The PI asks if she helped with any of the college fees, to which the stepmom cackles and denies giving "the tramp" any money. He then states she must have taken loans and then made up the rest with her work-study program, working at the campus library.

The stepmom rolls her eyes. "The library, huh? Well, I don't believe that."

I ask her about the patient's remains and the fact that the hospital told us she had claimed them.

"Oh, yes, they kept calling me. So I eventually picked them up. I have them." And she points to a white box in a clear bag sitting in the corner. "I am not certain what to do with them."

I ask about a memorial service, and she replies with another raspy laugh.

She puts out her butt. "A memorial? I don't have a clue if she had any friends, and if she did, well, I wouldn't want to host a bunch of panting Johns. Honestly, I was thinking of setting the ashes out with the trash; that's probably where she belongs."

I am horrified. Can you just put someone's remains in the trash?

She keeps rambling. "I had to go to her apartment to pick up her things. Luckily it was a furnished efficiency, so there wasn't much. I put all of her clothes"—she has a look of disgust—"that revealing crap she wore, in bags and donated them to Goodwill, though I doubt anyone would want that crap. I am glad she was subleasing and there wasn't any place to put me as a cosigner. Can you imagine if they tried to hit me up for her rent? Hah!" She lights another cigarette. "I have her phone; it's a pay as you go, if you want to see it?"

The PI nods, and she is ready with the phone on a nearby table, and she hands it to him. He immediately starts looking through the phone, and then without asking, he connects it to a laptop that seems to be extracting data.

"And then there's this baby crap. It all looks pretty cheap to me." She motions to the collection of baby items. There's a bassinette and an umbrella stroller, a few outfits and some diapers. "That's the only stuff I took from her apartment. I figured I'd have a yard sale...unless you would want it?" She takes a long drag on her cigarette. "How about a hundred dollars for the entire lot?"

I shrug somewhat indifferently. I go over and browse the few items. I suppose I could use them, but honestly, they are not even worth one hundred dollars, total. Most of it does appear on the cheaper side, but to me it shows that the mom was making an effort. The items are useful, even if they are the bare basics. I don't want to seem rude. I pick out one outfit. I figure it will be a small memorial to the mom, and I offer five dollars.

"How about ten dollars, and I'll throw in the diapers."

The diapers are generic, and though I don't know a thing about choosing diapers, they are probably just fine. The truth is that I don't want to give this woman anything. I look over at the remains sitting in the corner.

Through a clear bag, I can see a label with her name (last, first, DOB, DOD) on a white box, about the size of a shoe box, the current place of her remains.

"Are you really going to put her remains in the trash?"

She's apathetic. "I don't know what else to do with them."

I look at the PI, who periodically takes notes from the phone but is aware of our conversation. I ask him if it's allowed to dump someone's ashes. He looks at me and says, "Well, if her death is documented and if you get permission from the dumpsite, I think so."

"No, that can't be possible!" I shout. "Let me take the remains—if I get the child, she may want to see them someday."

"God only knows why you would want that child. I mean, you don't know what that child has. I am probably not at liberty to say, but I certainly have my suspicions!" the stepmom says, continuing to smoke.

I guess people might think I am crazy. I know what she has, and I want the child.

The stepmom seems to get an idea. "Hmmm, maybe you could take them ashes off of my hands, for, say, five hundred dollars."

The PI looks up startled and shakes his head in an obvious no gesture.

"But, if you're just going to throw them away..." I plead.

"Oh, she was trash. Sometimes it's hard for me to believe that she was the offspring of my late husband." She takes a puff. "He was such a good man."

"So I am guessing that you wouldn't want updates on the child. I could send you photos." I am thinking how my list of questions that I made up in the café is so absurd now.

"Oh, God, no! What do I care about that little bastard?"

"But your daughter is her half—"

"No, she is not half of anything to her. We want nothing to do with that little bastard. Is that clear?"

I nod.

She exhales. "Look, give me one hundred a fifty dollars, and you can have all of this stuff and her remains. That way I can wash my hands of that little hussy and her bastard baby."

What I want to do is slap her, but I keep thinking of the baby and if I could give her a chance to have her biological mom's remains. That might really mean something to the baby someday, no matter who or what her mom was. I offer her one hundred dollars for everything.

The PI gives me a cautious glare.

She taps her cigarette on the ashtray.

I add, "Then you will be clear of all of this."

She nods.

I am so thankful I have cash. I would not want to give this woman any more information about myself. I can't say much about the woman whose ashes are in the box, but the stepmom is evil.

The PI helps me load the few items into my car. I put the box in the passenger side and strap her in with the seatbelt. The PI is speechless, but he just pats me on the back and gives a knowing nod. He says he will follow up on some of the phone numbers and then call me.

Driving home, I am shaking and tearful. I look at my passenger, and I understand her pathetic life.

At home I put the baby gear in the room with the crib. I tear off tags and wash the clothes. I put the diapers by the spare sheets in the closet. And I put the ashes on the mantle. I tell her I am sorry and that I will get her a nice box.

It might be hard to explain why I have a stranger's ashes on my mantle if I don't bring this baby home...

No, I will.

I am reminded of the ashes of the twins. I remember the similar, nondescript white boxes. My ex-husband picked out urns. We had a small ceremony, and the urns were buried. I never thought to bring them home. I wasn't thinking much, then.

I look around the house and garage as if I might just have a decorative box sitting around.

As I suspected, I don't have one, or any box that I could decorate, or even anything to decorate a box if I had one.

I decide to run to the hobby store to find a box. And then I'll go to a pizza buffet restaurant and have pizza and beer. Beer sounds so good right now.

I spend far too much time in the hobby store looking at boxes and vases. I think a vase, urn, might be nice, but then I will have to move the ashes somehow, and that doesn't appeal to me. I just want a box to put them—no, her in that looks respectable. Then I start thinking about a label or labeling process, and then I realize I am overthinking the whole thing, but by then, I have found all sorts of cute items to make a young daughter's room very girly. I let my fingers touch the pink frilly items. Some are tasteful things like feet with ballet shoes, faces with freckles, hair with ribbons and bows. Others are less so, like a glittery "PRINCESS" sign. I'm not sure how, but without touching the sign, some of the glitter springs onto my hands and clothing. I brush it away as best as I can, but then I note sparkles on my pants. Definitely no glitter, but something to soften the room with a crib would be nice. So tempting, but then I worry about further inspections and constantly being judged for correctness and safety. I wonder if the scrutiny will ever end. I just gather ideas in my head for now, and I leave with an adequate-appearing box.

The pizza place is jumping with families. I wonder why I never noticed that before. Probably because I am usually here late grabbing the last bits of pizza before they clean up the buffet. I get my usual, a buffet and a beer on tap. I love to get more pizza than I ever need to eat in one sitting. I love the beer in a frosty mug. It goes down so cool and smooth. I watch the game; which game, I really don't know.

On my way home, I consider calling my parents. I am too emotional, and they would know something is wrong. They don't need to worry about me.

When I get home, I go straight to the mantle. The remains fit fine in the box without any adjusting, but then they sit precariously, as the box is a little deeper than the mantle. So I move her to a shelf in a half-empty book shelf.

I sleep fitfully with vivid dreams. What am I wearing? The material is a coarse weave of a neutral color, shapeless; the sleeping gown fits much like a potato sack, but it's surprisingly comfortable. I lie on my side, and my breathing is heavy. Whoa! I am pregnant. I have a full belly with tight skin. I startle and feel a kick. I sense I am old, older than I am now, but I still want to be pregnant.

I hear a rustle. Where am I? The bed is rustic, not very hygienic. There are no covers, but the environment is warm. The room is dim, maybe nearing dawn. There's a cool breeze and a damp quality to the air. Where am I?

A set of individuals, I think three, in clean white attire enter the room. They roll a futuristic-looking ultrasound into the room. One of them starts up the scanner. The machine buzzes softly, then flickers and whirs. One lifts my soft and simple gown up to reveal my full belly. I am not afraid. The familiar, cool gel drops onto my belly, foreign, but familiar. She places the transducer on my lower abdomen. The others just stand by and witness. Wavy lines and bright rays produce a picture in a curvilinear shape. There is a baby in my womb. I see the amniotic fluid, the legs, the abdomen with bladder and stomach. Moving upward, we see the spine, then the chest with the heart and dark, fluid-filled lungs, then moving up further we find the head with the face and cranium. Shown at the top of his head is a radiant halo. The two standing by nod in acknowledgment and smile.

Whoa, that was strange! I awake in bewilderment. What a bizarre dream!

It reminds me of the peculiar dreams I had when I was pregnant and how I would awake to remember some weird, unbelievable vision of pregnancy, like the dream where I was having twins and there was no doctor, or anyone, around to deliver the babies. I can't recall why there were no doctors around. I just found myself in a room, in a labor and delivery ward, and no one was around. I remember feeling labor, feeling the pain, and screaming. I screamed for help only to have had silence answer. Again I can't say why the room was a perfect labor and delivery room with every necessity except people; that's just where I appeared. The circumstances are a little fuzzy, but I was alone. I had no choice; I had to deliver them myself. In that dream, the babies were born full-term and alive. I had not yet given birth in my real life, but in my dream I perceived childbirth: the waves of pain, the breathing, the pushing and praying. I sensed the stretching and the emergence of each child. As the first child's head crowned, I guided the head as best as I could. After the head, I breathed and then pushed, then the body with a burst of warm water birthed on the bed. I looked down at the newborn. I can't really recall the baby distinctively, other than just a generic healthy newborn. The visual memory is less clear, but the feelings of pride and instant love are indelible. Supplies were readily at hand to cut the cord, to suction the newborn's nose, and to swaddle the baby in blankets. I placed the baby on a dry spot on the bed, still between my legs. I braced myself for the next baby. The waves of contractions returned with the pain. Again, I screamed for help, "Please, somebody help me! Please, somebody. Aaaaah!" No one replied. More pain and trepidation; I knew too much about delivering twins and the difficulty of delivering the second child. I felt my belly to discern the position of the second baby. I realized that the baby was lengthwise up and down, and not transverse, which would have been near impossible to deliver, except perhaps in a dream. The contractions regulated, bringing about more prayers and screaming for help. "I can do this," I tried to convince myself. I continued to scream, in pain and for help. The second bag of water burst, and the first baby's blanket was splashed. No time to think, I felt for the head. I could feel the baby moving down. I pushed with all my might. The second was mercifully quicker to deliver, and came out all at once with little coaxing. I cut the cord, suctioned the nose, and swaddled the second little bundle. I sat some blankets down to absorb some of the wetness and then laid both babies side by side in between my legs. I wanted so much to hold them, but my tasks were not yet finished. Next the fused placentas delivered, and I placed them in a metal pan. Lastly, I remember, I had to sew myself up looking in a mirror, the only truly visual aspect of the dream. The mirror simply existed at the end of the bed. Everything I needed, a tray with all the necessary stainless wares and sutures, was just in my reach. I am stupefied that I didn't awaken at delivery, but rather, it was driving the needle through my torn perineum that alarmed me to awaken. Instinctively, I reached for my belly, which was full. Little kicks gave me a sense of reassurance; though the cold sweat, maybe, should have told me otherwise.

The memory of that dream affects me even now. I'll never forget that dream, and I don't suppose I'll ever forget this one either.

I reflexively touch my belly, which is flat, or rather, not pregnant. There is no chance that I could be pregnant right now, or it would have to be an immaculate conception. I laugh and think, "Well, that would explain the halo."

Today is another work day. I am up early and regardless of my weird awakening, I am in a good mood to go to the hospital again. Of course, I visit the baby. I feel happy, and it seems that other people at the hospital are happy too.

Be late.

The next day, my lawyer calls with good news. He and the guardian have arranged a meeting with the judge tomorrow to discuss and approve my fost-adopt, or at the least, my guardianship. We will meet informally with the judge in his chambers. He will need to go over my whole record, so if I want to get there thirty to forty-five minutes after they start, that would be advisable.

"Thirty to forty-five minutes late? No, of course I want to be there for the whole event."

"Uh, I am actually recommending that you get there a little late. I need to present your record and get a feel of the judge's mood," the lawyer answers.

"But I don't want to seem indifferent."

"Listen, you will not seem indifferent. Trust me, you have gotten your whole record together in less than two weeks; you are not indifferent. I need you to get there a little late. If you arrive on time, the judge may have you sit out for a while anyway. This gives us time to discuss your case. Just trust me," he pleads. "And if you do get there early, go get a cup of coffee or be elsewhere for a while."

I take all of this in and question why he just didn't tell me the meeting started later than it does. I get a shock. "Is it possible the judge won't accept my case?"

There is an unsettling pause. "My only concern is that two weeks may not show a dedicated interest, but my feeling is that you are a good match, and I think the guardian has the same feelings." He adds, "You have a lot going for you. In your records, I have a statement from the hospital administrator and social worker recommending you highly, and surprisingly, you seem to have dazzled the social worker who did your home visit. Seriously, I don't know how you did that. Furthermore, your psychological evaluation shows someone who can remain focused and stay calm in the face of bad circumstances."

All of this is amazingly good news, but I still feel intimidated.

He continues, "I'll see if the judge will accept the fost-adopt, but there will probably be some strings attached."

"Meaning?"

"Meaning, you will probably have many more follow-up home visits from the social worker. You might have to attend more baby care and child care classes. Or he may have some waiting period, but this is unlikely, as there is no one else to take the child at this time. I expect you and the social worker, or antisocial worker as I like to call her, will become close friends for a while."

"Does she ever get any better?"

"A little, but she is always a bit abrasive."

"Are you sure I shouldn't be there at the beginning? If he has questions about me, shouldn't I be the one to answer them?"

"Hmmm, how do I get this through to you? If you were reading about someone's life and back ground, would you want that person standing over you?"

I have to think about this.

"Maybe I didn't put that exactly right, but just come forty-five minutes late. You will probably be sitting outside the chambers anyway, and then you will be called in."

I realize he's taken out the thirty-minute option. "This sounds stressful."

"Remember, I've done this before. We will get through it."

"And if we don't?" I think, but I say, "Okay."

The courthouse...

All night I am thinking of things to say, possible answers to questions I might be asked.

In the morning I take a while to pick out what to wear. I settle on slacks and a blouse. I wear sensible shoes, comfortable and nothing that I might wobble in if I get shaky, and a belt and a scarf for color. What am I forgetting? Do I need a notebook? It seems that holding something might settle my hands, but I don't have a suitable notebook. I'd better get going. Even trying to be late, I am on time. I park and sit in my car. I note a deli across the street, but coffee will not help my tension. I check e-mails and texts as I sit in my car.

The PI has texted this morning at 9:14 a.m.:

"When you get a chance, call me."

Well, I have a chance, so I call.

The PI starts with, "I am glad you called. I have many updates that might make a difference in your decision making." He presses on, "I went to her campus and spoke with her professors. None of them seemed to know her very well. Two professors were in large amphitheater classes, one is an online professor, and the last professor ran a small class, but he couldn't say much about her or her friends. As for classmates, I went to most of her classes and tried to get the kids to speak, but no one that I ran into could say more than, 'Oh yeah, I think she was in this class.' I was getting nowhere, until I met with her counselor. Of course, he couldn't divulge much, but he did say that she seemed to fall into a bad group of friends. He hinted that occasionally he would find a girl stripping to work through school, or worse. He said he helped her get the job at the library. He knew she was pregnant and was trying to help steer her in the right direction, but she hadn't visited him in a while."

"You could find out if she was a stripper, right?"

"Yeah, and she wasn't, at least not at any of the main places in town."

"How do you know?" Oh, man, am I paying him to go to strip joints?

"I have connections. I made calls." He sounds anxious to give me more information.

"So it was worse?"

"Yeah, running through her cell phone, most of the numbers are now disconnected. And looking at sites on the Internet, it seems she probably solicited herself in that way."

"Did you find proof?"

"Sometimes the lack of proof is the proof, but in this case, she had some money exchange with an online company that runs such ads. I wasn't able to pull up past ads, but the current ads are pretty telling. Then there's her phone. There were a few numbers that were still running, like her school, her doctor's office, her stepmom. But then she would have groupings of calls to a specific telephone number for about a week, and then you wouldn't see that number ever again. But there would be a new number she would call repetitively for a week, and then that number would disappear and so on. You see this with girls who use pimps or some service; their numbers roll over a lot. They're often prepaid numbers, and they continually change them. It's part of the game. Actually, I'm surprised she had this phone and phone number as long as she did." Rushing through her story, the PI's voice is becoming raspier and breathier.

"Are you sure? I mean, her obstetrician said she told him the father was a ball player, maybe football or basketball."

"I am pretty sure. I do not think you will find the father. As for him being a ball player, she may have just made that up, or who knows. There are lots of different guys that use prostitutes."

Use. That's a good word for it. "Wouldn't she have used condoms?"

"I can't answer that for sure, but you're the expert, right? Condoms aren't foolproof."

"Yeah, that's true." Well, there it is. "What's next then?"

"Well, you paid me half up front, for two weeks, and I've done about a week of work, so I think we're even."

"Do you think there's anything else to learn or look for?"

"No, I think that about sums it up. You will not find a father. I am certain about that. Sometimes among the numbers that roll over you'll find a few that stay that belong to close friends, but there aren't any, other than the few I mentioned."

"I know she used some drugs. Could those numbers be to and from a drug dealer?"

"Could be, but I thought my job was mostly to look for a dad or any relative that might come forward to claim the baby, and basically, I am telling you there is no one, in my opinion of doing this job for over thirty years, no one who is going to come forward and claim that baby."

"Right, I guess I was getting off track a bit." I am uneasy with his explanation. "Could you really assess all of that just from her cell phone? How far could you look back? I mean, she was pregnant seven to eight months."

"You can pull up several months of calls on a cell phone, more if they don't make so many calls. Also, it helps to have someone at different carriers who might be able to help look up past records, not that I know someone like that. If you know what I mean?"

I start scrolling through calls on my cell phone, and I am amazed to pull up four months of prior phone calls. While mesmerized with my phone, I say, "Thank you. So I guess I just call you if I need anything further?"

"Yes, ma'am, and I'll send you a finalized receipt and write-up of all findings, or would you rather I send that to your lawyer?"

Lawyer… "Uh, just send it to me; I need to go. Thanks so much."

I hang up, and I rush out of the car, grabbing my purse, and run into the courthouse, where there is a long line to get through a metal detector. Oh, crap! The line takes fifteen minutes. By the time I find the chambers, I am almost a full hour late. I speak to a woman at a desk, who tells me to have a seat.

I have to go to the bathroom, but I don't know when I will be called. I ask the woman at the desk, and she advises me to go to the bathroom. "Don't worry. If they come out looking for you, I will tell them I'll send you in as soon as you come back."

I get back just as they are calling me in. My lawyer meets me first and says he hopes I wasn't waiting too long.

I just smile and try not to sound nervous when I say, "No, not too long."

I enter the chamber, which is essentially an office with dark paneling, a large wooden desk, and chairs. The only notable difference is the large flags on either side of the desk. The judge sitting behind the desk stands and shakes my hand. I also shake hands with the guardian and tell her it's good to see her again. The judge motions us all to have seats.

The judge summarizes my whole case and ends asking, "You would therefore like to adopt this baby?"

"Yes, I would."

"Well, we have discussed your case, and I am a little concerned about the two- to three-week timeline."

My insides turn over, and I am certain everyone hears their sound.

"On the other hand, you have wonderful recommendations. You have stable work and no debts. Your background check is completely negative. Your home report is favorable. You seem to have a sound mind." He strokes his beard. "I have decided that you will be the foster mom for this child. You will have home visits at one week and then every three months for a year, and then at two years. If at the end of one year, the child is thriving in your home and there are no other claims on the child, then you will formally adopt the child. If there are any concerns, this can be delayed until two years." He looks directly at me.

Only now, in this brief pause of silence, do I notice a court recorder typing his every word.

I hear that I am going to foster the child, and I feel relieved, but then the two-year trial period puts me on edge. I feel his gaze adding to my emotional uncertainty; relieved, revealed. I calm myself thinking, I will do whatever it takes.

"Does this seem acceptable to everyone here?" the judge queries.

We all agree.

We leave the courthouse, and my lawyer says, "It's customary, and it would be my pleasure to take you out to lunch to celebrate."

Only then does it really sink in.

Over lunch, at a little French bistro, I tell him about the findings of the PI.

"Well, he had told me about your visit with the stepmom. That sounded like a horror story!" He looks a bit like Frankenstein with claws and bold eyes as he says this.

I love how he can turn off his gesticulations for business and how they rebound afterward. "Yes, it was a bit of a horror story. Did the PI tell you all about it? Do you know I have her ashes?"

"Yes, the stepmom sold them to you. Sold or whatever you would call the transaction. Because of the possible legal ramifications of the sale of remains, if there are any, I am going to say that you bought the baby items, and she *gave* you the remains, for the sake of the baby. By the way, you did the right thing." After a slight pause, he changes the topic. "I guess you never saw her daughter, huh? I mean her biological daughter. She was at school, right?"

I nod.

"I am wondering if I shouldn't have a social worker interview her to make sure CPS doesn't need to be involved, but then again, stepdaughter versus daughter"—he holds his hands out like a balance—"that can make a world of difference." One hand goes up and the other down.

I just nod.

"A prostitute, huh? You're not upset about that or think less of your daughter or having any second thoughts?"

"No," and I tell him of visiting the baby in the nursery and how I turn into a happy mush around her.

With that, he orders champagne.

I am not sure if I am paying, and I don't care.

A week later, I bring my daughter home.

During that week, I am industrious.

I sign papers with my lawyer. I pay him, and though it's a lot for the brief amount of time, he is worth it. Why would I have ever questioned my brother's recommendation?

I meet with the neonatologist and learn about medicines and care of a baby. He helps me find a pediatrician and signs my family leave papers.

I arrange to be off work for five weeks, and I call in all my favors for other doctors to work my shifts.

I arrange for the baby to be on my health insurance.

I go back to the baby megamart with more confidence.

I paint and decorate the room yellow with lavender polka dots. Very whimsical! Even painting feels carefree. The dots vary in size, shape, and location, but it winds up looking fun! I think my lawyer would be impressed.

I call my brother and I tell him everything. He says he will visit. I ask him how to tell our parents. He gives me some advice.

I call to tell my parents. I don't tell them everything. They ask me tons of questions. When did all of this happen? Why didn't you tell us sooner? How do you plan on raising a child on your own? Is the baby okay? How did the mom die? How well do you know this woman? Was she on drugs? Did she have any diseases? What about a father? A preemie, don't they have long-term problems like retardation? If you wanted a daughter, why didn't you adopt a child from China? I answer them as vaguely as I can. Finally: when will we meet her?

I'm certain as soon as I get off the phone with my mom that she is calling everyone she knows, and my ears are burning.

She is my foster daughter...

On the day of discharge, when I go to get the baby, the hospital staff surprises me with a baby shower. So many of the staff are there that you would think that there wasn't a hospital to run. We stand outside of the NICU, in the NICU waiting area. As I look around, I know all of the faces, the innumerable nurses from different units, the anesthesia staff, other OBs, a few pediatricians and neonatologists, operating room staff, the social worker, and some administrators.

The administrator even says a few words of kindness. "We all have known this good doctor for a long time, some good times and some not so good times, but she's always been a hard worker, helpful in times of need." There are some nods and smiles in response. "She's always nice and compassionate, even during difficult cases. She is one of our own, stepping up to the plate to take on an infant in need, and we wish you all the best!"

There's a brief moment of applause. Maybe my silent sorrow was interpreted as quiet diligence. They sit me down to open a few gifts. There aren't too many. I get diapers and formula, a thermometer, a few cute outfits, a blanket, a few wash cloths, and a hooded towel. Many gifts look like they were purchased from the hospital gift shop that now also sells gift bags preloaded with tissue paper, so the wrappings also look familiar. We are a busy, but well-meaning group, and the gift shop is our default convenience store. I am touched that someone had a reason to buy me a baby gift from the hospital gift shop, as I have done from time to time for others. I read the gift cards with tender sayings of encouragement for all I've been through, most followed by multiple signatures:

"We were rooting for you all the way!

Congratulations!"

From the Neo Team

"It's so nice to see you happy!

Best Wishes!"

The Nurses of Unit C

"You make us proud!

Best wishes and happy parenting!"

Administration

"Congratulations!"

Anesthesia and OR Staff

"There were so many times I wanted to reach out to you. When you finally made it into my office, I knew I needed to help you. I know you will be a great mom!

Signed, SW

(P.S. Call if you need anything! Tel: ###-###-####)

The last one from the social worker almost has me in tears. I guess she really did know me after all.

I sign the discharge papers, and I am treated like a mom being discharged with her baby from the hospital. They put me in a wheelchair with my daughter on my lap. I am grateful that someone is taking pictures and tells me she will e-mail them to me. They get a cart to help me with all my presents and load them into my car. They check the baby car seat, buckle the baby in, and wish us well.

I love my hospital family; they are the most unobtrusive and compassionate people.

I check the baby and close the rear door. From the driver's seat, I roll down the window and give another round of thanks. I notice the social worker smiling and waving.

I drive home very cautiously with my precious cargo.

When I get home, I'm in for another huge surprise. My brother and my mom and dad are there in the driveway. I can't believe it. In some ways, I was looking forward to some alone time to bond with my daughter, but they are my family, and I am sure they are anxious to meet her.

They wave at us. I park very slowly, trying to buy a little time before the interrogation begins. I take a deep breath before emerging from the vehicle. The baby is asleep. My parents rush toward the vehicle and hug me.

"Oh, can we see her?" my mom asks.

I pop open the trunk, reach in, and grab the metal gizmo. My mom has already opened the rear car door, and my parents are bending in to study the baby.

"If you let me get her out, I can put the car seat on this so she doesn't wake up," I say, hoping she doesn't wakeup.

They back away, and I wedge the frame against the open door. I unclick the baby seat from the car base and then click it into the stroller device. I also grab the diaper bag and my purse and place them in the netting below. I aim to look like I know what I am doing. I wheel her outward and turn her around to face the family. My brother closes the car door and peers at the baby over my shoulder.

"Oh, she's so tiny!" my mom squeals. "So tiny! She's so calm. She's a little slumped over, but she's breathing okay; right, she's pink and has pretty, full lips."

They ooh and ah! I am brimming with pride.

"Oh, we should go inside. Let's move out of the driveway, huh?" My mom is directing.

I push the stroller to the door, and I am careful going over the door plate.

My parents follow me in, but my brother has gone back to my parents' car and withdraws a giant basket with a pink bow. He follows, grinning behind the massive offering.

Through the cellophane, the basket holds diapers, formula, a bathing kit, socks, and other baby items.

My brother kids that he wishes he had a stroller to click the basket into so it would be easier to handle. Once inside, he sets the basket down.

My mom admonishes him. "I am sorry. We didn't know what you might need, and so, well, they were so very helpful at the baby megamart that before I knew it, I had loaded an entire cart. I didn't know how I would get it all here, and they offered to wrap it for me in a big bassinette." She is very pleased, and she points to the basket. "You see, it's not just a basket, but a bassinette. See, it's lined with a soft covering. Then they wrapped it all up so cute. Well, you wouldn't believe how efficient and amazing the place is!" My mom seems completely satisfied.

"Oh, I know how helpful they are," I agree.

"I mean for just a little bit more, they wrapped it all up. Well, it's sensational! Not that they had to talk me into much. I thought, for my first and possibly only grandchild..." She pauses and ponders aloud, "She is yours, right? I mean, how certain are you?"

My dad tries to hush her.

"She is mine," I say defensively.

My brother gives me a big hug.

My parents look at my daughter, and my mom continues commenting. "She's so quiet. Is she okay?"

I am sensing this is more than a simple question, but I simply reply, "Yes."

"Well, you could have told us sooner. Couldn't you have told your parents sooner?"

I am feeling belittled in a way that only a parent can make you feel. I am almost tearful, but I reply, "She is only three to four weeks old, and you have no idea all that I have done to—" And it hits me, all I have done, the exhaustive marathon since she was born. "I crammed in legal visits, a home inspection, a parenting conference, multiple hospital conferences, and a hearing with a judge." Not to mention the PI and the stepmom visit, which I do not mention. "I began this all only a few weeks ago, and I am grateful for everyone who helped me, and she is home now. And now you know." I risk looking at my brother when I say that I am grateful.

My mom is still not satisfied with my answer. "I only heard a few days ago. It seems that your brother knew."

"*I* only knew a few days ago!" I interject. "A week to be exact," I add.

We are all standing inside, feeling awkward.

"How about those helpful associates at the baby megamart, huh?" my brother says, trying to lighten the mood a bit. "I noticed you have quite a few items in the car. Can I get them and bring them inside?"

"Yes, thanks," I reply.

My dad says he will help also, and the two men dart outside without hesitation.

"Thanks," I call after them, but this leaves my mother and me and the sleeping baby. "Why don't I wheel her into the living room, where we can sit?"

I had strategically placed my purse and baby bag onto the stroller before exiting the car. The baby bag has a month's worth of medicines for the baby, as the hospital knows that it can take time to get insurance for the baby, and they do not want any lapse in her medicines. I was also told I could get one more month's worth if necessary. I don't want to panic, but I can't let my parents look into that bag. When I get a chance, I'll stash it in my room somewhere.

My mom and I sit in the living room and watch the guys bring in their loads.

As if our silence isn't odd enough, I see that my mom eyes the box sitting on the shelf. Oh, please don't ask, please, please, please.

"Would you like me to get us all something to drink? What do you have? Maybe I could make some tea?"

"Oh, that would be great, Mom. There's a pitcher of iced tea in the refrigerator. And I have a lemon somewhere."

My dad and brother finish with their loads and sit down.

"Mom is getting us all iced tea. If you want something else, let her know," I say. I am trying to think of something I can say that is in the decorative box, without raising suspicion or a desire to look inside. I can't think of anything, and I realize I'd better just stick with the truth—but only if anyone asks. Well, the half-truth, where the stepmom graciously—oh no, I'd better not mention the stepmom. I simply requested the remains for the sake of the baby…um, remember KISS, and just answer the question. They are the remains of the baby's mom, and then if they ask why, then I will tell them that I requested the remains for the sake of the baby.

My mom brings in the beverages. As we sit there and sip our tea, I look around at all the items. My living room has never been so full, or so lived in.

We examine the baby items I got from the hospital, and I have another mini-shower. My mom has a comment for every item, and for some items she has several comments. She asks me if I have a list of who gave me what so I can write thank-you notes.

My dad pulls out a newspaper, from where, I have no idea. He starts to read.

I don't answer my mom's question, and I resist the urge to roll my eyes. She doesn't ask again.

My brother asks if he can stay and help. "I mean, actually stay here. My bags are still in their car."

"That would be great." I am thinking how if he stays, it will be easier to tell him about being a backup parent, maybe even ask him to be a godfather. I also realize that I am saving him from having to stay at home.

My mom also offers to stay and help. "You know that babies are a lot of work?" Without letting me answer, she says, "I can't believe it! You are a mom! You are now a mom, and so suddenly. I feel like you and your brother have a secret that you're not telling us, like your dad and I are outside of the loop. I mean, we are all here, including your brother. You are a mom, and I am a grandma! Oh my goodness!"

"Mom, um..." I am not sure how to decline her question.

My dad looks up from the paper. "You know, honey, maybe you could help after he's gone home. That way she's not so crowded. And there's that thing you want to ask her," he prompts.

"Oh, yes, well, I haven't told anyone."

My dad clears his throat. "Correction. You haven't told *everyone*," my dad says from behind the paper.

"Well, I just don't want the news out until we know she's really, uh, yours, um, part of our family," my mom stumbles.

"Too late. I fear the news is out." Again the newspaper speaks.

"Well, it's just, if you are sure, then some of my friends would like to throw you a baby shower." She smiles. "If that's okay with you?"

"Okay, but maybe in a few weeks." I can imagine my mom has only told a few of her closest friends, which means that all of her friends know, because none of them can keep a secret.

"Oh, well, of course, it's not like we could plan a shower overnight." She smiles desperately. "I mean, we have to pick out stationery and order invitations, and—"

We hear a sigh and the turning of a page of the newspaper.

"Well, it's true," my mom retorts.

We are silent for a while, and then my brother pulls out his phone. "I am going to film some, if that's okay? I mean, we have a new member of the family!"

We all wave at the camera and smile and talk about her birthday and her coming to the house and how we are all very excited, and we welcome her to the family. Somehow being on video puts us all on our best behavior. See, we are all a loving family! We even take her on a stroll to "see" her new bedroom; the baby continues to sleep.

My mom says to the baby, "Oh look, sweetie. Just look at your bedroom!"

I almost expect my mom to comment on the colors and how they clash, but no, she is on camera and all smiles!

The baby is asleep.

"Well, what's her name?" my dad asks, still seated in the living room, somehow following the whole conversation from behind the paper.

"I haven't decided yet. I like the idea of Hope, but I'm not sure if it's corny." When I was pregnant with the twins, I was going to name the girl Chloe or Zoe, but that doesn't feel right. No one responds. "So I guess you don't like Hope?"

"I like it," my brother says from behind the camera.

I give him a questioning look.

"Well, it's whatever you decide," he says.

"Would anyone like to give their input?" I dare ask.

"I like June or Charlotte or maybe Clara," my mom says.

Of course she has an opinion. The baby startles and cries.

"Don't worry, I won't call you Clara," I say, but she gets all the attention.

"Oh, look, I think she's rooting. She's hungry. What do you plan on feeding her?" my mom asks.

I think about making a joke about cat food, but I don't. "I'll get a bottle." I carefully remove the baby bag from below the buggy.

My mom pushes the stroller back to the living room, and my brother follows, still filming off and on.

"Oh, can I take her out and hold her?" my mom asks. "Oh, Grandma is here, darling, and don't worry, I won't call you Hope." She looks at me sheepishly. Then she unbuckles little Hope and cradles her in her arms. She looks into her eyes and makes cooing noises.

The hospital gave me twelve premade bottles. I pull one out of the bag, shake and open it, and place a nipple on the top. I hand it to my mom.

"But this isn't warmed!" she scoffs.

"I don't think they warm them at the hospital." I am really not sure; I try to recall the few times I fed her in the hospital. No, I never used warmed milk when feeding her there.

Reluctantly, my mom takes the bottle from me and starts feeding the baby, "Okay, maybe Grandma has a bit to learn." She sits with the infant in her lap. "And I am kidding about Hope." She looks down at the child, "Yes, Hope might just fit, but it's hard to match a middle name with Hope. I mean, Hope June or Hope Charlotte. What do you put behind Hope?"

"How about Hopeful Charlotte," my brother offers jokingly.

"I kind of like it." I am serious, but my brother laughs.

As my mom feeds Hope, I take a moment to sort out the baby bag. I place the premade bottles in the kitchen and then stash the bag in a corner.

Later my mom offers to cook dinner. "What should we all have? I mean, it's a sort of celebration, and I can send your dad out for whatever we feel like, maybe even some champagne! Well, that's the good thing about not nursing; even the new mom can have a toast!" She pauses, tilts her head, and thinks aloud, "Actually, I heard that even moms who adopt can take hormones and nurse. Have you heard that?"

"Yes, but I think you need some time for the hormones to take effect, and I didn't have time to plan that, nor do I think that I will."

"Okay, good, then we will have some champagne!" She seems to be calculating in her head. "Well, what should we eat?"

My mom prepares a little list and sends my dad on his way. My dad happily obliges. I notice that before leaving he inspects the baby's bedroom on his way to the bathroom.

My brother follows my dad out to the car but returns with his luggage. "Okay if I put these in the spare bedroom?" he says as he passes me on the way there.

I nod and smile at him as he passes.

Later, my mom is cooking, and my dad is snoring behind his newspaper. I think newspapers could have been small booklets, but then men demanded something larger that they could hide behind.

At dinner I place the stroller at a place beside me, but so that the baby is facing the table. She is still pretty sleepy.

My dad pours champagne and also opens a bottle of wine and places it at the table. My mom puts serving pieces with food on the table. I hope she washed the dust off first.

My dad makes a toast, "To family."

"Well, is that all?" my mom remarks.

"Would you like to add something, dear?" My dad knows she does.

"I would like to welcome baby Hope to our family. We will always love you and take care of you." She seems to want to add more, but then she raises her glass.

Not bad, Mom. We all sip the champagne.

We eat, and it is nice having the family together.

After dinner, my brother cleans up, and my mom and I take inventory. She helps me open her basket/bassinette. My mom digs into her purse and pulls out the baby list from the baby megamart; she checks off what we already have. She also makes a separate list of the gift givers so I can be sure to send thank-you notes. She notes the maker, model, and wood selection of the crib and writes the colors, yellow and lavender.

My brother joins us, but when the baby cries, he jumps up to feed her.

"Aw, you're such a good uncle." My mom says, and then she gets down to business. "Okay, so you still need a changing station, a glider, a swing, a bouncer, burp cloths, onesies, receiving blankets, bibs…and of course you could always use more formula and diapers. The lady at the baby megamart told me not to buy bumpers or a mobile. Oh, look on the list; there's a bottle warmer. Huh." She gives me a glance.

"Okay, Mom."

"How many washrags did you get, and only one hooded towel? You will need more of those."

"I could always just use a regular towel or washcloth."

To this she wrinkles her nose. "Oh, honey, don't joke around. Now, do you want to help register for items, or would you like me to take care of it? Or do you just want a general list with a color scheme to stick to?"

"Um."

"Oh, a little girl! The opportunity for cute clothing is endless!" She can't contain herself. She looks at Dad asleep on the couch. "Maybe Grandpa should buy the matching glider, and then the shower hosts can buy the changing table. Oh, do you think you can wait that long? Maybe I'll see if they will buy it in advance, and we can just make an announcement at the shower."

I wonder if I can decline the shower offer now. "Mom, is there any way you and your closer friends could throw a smaller shower? You know, less formal, and then I could get those few things now?"

"Do you mean in addition to the larger shower?"

"No, I just meant something smaller and less formal."

"What? No, no. Don't you understand that those ladies owe me a shower?"

I shake my head. "What?"

"Do you know how many showers I have hosted or attended? And some of these ladies have several grandchildren. They owe me!" she says emphatically. "No, no. This may be my one chance and my one grandchild and, quite frankly, there are some ladies who have been dying to throw me a baby shower for years. I mean, for you of course. And you are behind the pack. I mean, you are forty-three years old; most of my friends' grandchildren are teenagers by now. Which is another reason to hold a shower; this is probably one of our last baby showers now that all of our kids are past the baby stage. Seriously, honey, this is important to me and my friends; we live for these events."

I want to say something to the effect about how it is all about my mom and her friends, but I know it's of no use. "We will have a shower." She pats my hand, and I tell her she can set up the registry, and when the day arrives, Hope and I will attend. We will be grateful.

Somehow, my mom is exhausting. Her next order of business is to prepare meals for me. She wants to know what I would like, and she will bring foods over tomorrow to prepare and freeze. "Oh, you will see. Having a quick meal to take out and prepare, you will thank me!"

My dad finally awakens and asks what time it is. My parents agree that it is getting late.

My mom grabs her few items to get going. She says I can call her at any time if I have questions, and she will get here early tomorrow with or without groceries; she can always send Dad out later. "That might be better." She agrees she will pick up bagels on the way and then send my dad to get groceries after breakfast.

My dad hugs me and says he is proud of me.

My mom hugs me and says, "I can't believe all of this. I just can't believe it! My daughter is a mom, and I barely had time to adjust." She kisses me and says, "Call if you need anything, and we will see you tomorrow!"

Then they are off.

My brother is still on the couch holding the baby. He says, "Hope. Are you sure about that?"

"No, I'm not exactly sure, but at least we can call her Hope for now."

"Well, why not Joy or Charity or Faith or Love?" he prods.

"I take it you don't like Hope?"

"I knew a pretty lady named Love. Well, she wasn't exactly a lady, but..."

"Oh, Mommy," I say in a girlish voice, "how was I named Love?" Then I change to an adult voice. "Well, honey, your uncle knew a pretty transvestite."

He rolls his eyes. "I was joking. Let's call her Hope, for now."

"I guess I should have bought a baby name book after all."

"Well, maybe when I need to escape tomorrow, I'll run out and get one."

"How about when I need to escape?" I retort.

"So how do we give her the medicines?" He says after a few silent moments.

"There are two medicines that I need to mix into her bottles twice a day, either together or separately. They said that I could mix them together, but if there's a reaction of some sort, I should separate the medicines so I can tell which medicine is causing it. Then there's an antibiotic that she needs to take Mondays, Wednesdays, and Fridays, or three times a week. I need to see her pediatrician in one week and her infectious disease specialist in a few days, and then I think they will alternate every week or so."

"Every week? For how long?"

"I am not sure, but I know she also needs blood work every so often."

"So do you have the meds, or do you need me to go get them?"

"The hospital sent me home with a month's supply." I explain why.

"How are you going to handle the medicines if mom stays over to help?"

I shake my head. "I have no idea. Maybe I can premix some bottles and line them up in the refrigerator."

"Hey, I noticed in the room with the crib that you already have a bassinette. Do you want mom to return the one she gave you?"

"No, I'll just put the one I have in the closet. It's funny that not much gets by mom, and she didn't mention the second bassinette."

"Oh, so will you return yours later?"

"Uh, no, that's not possible." I then relay the whole visit with the stepmom with my brother. "And that box there on the shelf has the mom's remains—ashes in it."

"No crap?"

"Hey, there's a young lady in the room." I point to the baby. "But, yes, no crap!"

"I saw mom noticed the box. What are you going to tell her if she asks?"

"I figure I will tell her the truth, that they are the ashes of Hope's biological mom."

"What will you tell her when she asks how you obtained them?"

"I will just tell her that no one else wanted them."

He smiles reassuringly. "You are going to be a good mom."

"I am not entirely sure what to think. It is almost impossible to believe that she is here. It feels like maybe she's not mine, but then she is. She is here."

"Do you think that you will ever mention to mom and dad that Hope may have HIV?"

"No, I don't think that—"

"But, I mean, they know about me and my partner, Angelo, who died. Maybe they can understand more than you might think?"

"Well, if it will get her to call off the shower, then maybe."

"No, really." He looks pretty sincere. "Mom's toast claimed we would always love and take care of Hope."

"That might be, but I worry more about Hope."

"Why?"

"Because Mom can't keep a secret, and Hope will have to grow up with everyone knowing her business."

"Is that so bad?"

"Truthfully, Mom's friends would just pity me and Hope, and then they would probably take up HIV as a new cause and reason for prayer, but at a distance, of course."

"But what about the medicines and doctors' visits, and what if you need help?" he continues.

"I just don't know right now." I know I am not going to tell my parents.

"I think you should just have a powwow with Mom and Dad and me," he offers. "You just spill the whole story, from the cesarean, the death of the mom with HIV, the stepmom, everything. Just get it all out there, no secrets, and I bet you will be amazed, impressed even."

"Seriously, a powwow." I look at him as though he has got to be crazy. "Mom and Dad will think I am nuts for taking on such a child."

"Do you know that Mom and Dad came to Angelo's funeral? And at the time, Mom was torn because she wasn't sure she should leave you when you were going through your divorce, not that you ever reached out to her."

"Why is that?"

"I don't know; you tell me."

"No, I mean, sons are always closer to their moms, and daughters are always at odds with their moms. I guess it's just human nature."

"Beware; you too now have a daughter."

"Are you sad I didn't make the funeral?"

"No, I was just sad."

I smile at his sincerity. "I hate to pry, but I know people can live many years on antiretrovirals, and I know Angelo had problems with his medicines, but what happened?"

"Oh, yes, for many people they do work, but in his case he couldn't take most of them. Somehow he was sensitive; his blood counts would drop, or his liver would become too toxic. He had some depression also; I think most people with HIV can't escape the depression. He didn't want to take even the few pills he was able to tolerate. He said they were just prolonging his miserable life." He pauses as if remembering a hopeless battle. "Slowly, the virus spread, even if I could get him to take a few medicines. The virus went into his brain, and he became a different person, lots of delusions and tremors and terrors, and it wasn't long after that."

"I remember you telling me he couldn't tolerate the medicines and that he was getting weaker, and then I heard about the funeral. I'm sorry I wasn't so supportive."

"No, the few times you called, you were fine."

"I think you were more supportive of me and my problems, which seem a little less now."

"How did Hope's mom die?"

"She fell to pneumonia, but she also didn't take her medicines. I don't really know why, but I think she probably also had some depression."

He nods with understanding. After a bit of quiet, he nudges, "What do you say we start mixing some bottles?"

"What do you think about calling her Angela?"

He smiles but shakes his head no.

"Hope Angela?" I propose.

He nods and says, "I'd like that, but you don't need to call her that if you don't want to."

"No, I think it's perfect. We will still call her Hope, and Angela can be her middle name."

With that, we go to the kitchen and set up an assembly line of syrups and formula. We label the bottles with numbers to know what order we need to give the bottles.

I'm so glad my brother is here to help me. "I need to ask you a question about Hope."

My brother looks up.

"I needed a contingency plan because I am a single mom, and so I put you down as...as um—"

"Yeah, I know. I had to sign papers."

"What?"

"Oh, yeah, the lawyer called me and told me your plan. He said you were at some weekend conference and couldn't be reached but that he needed the documents signed, and so he faxed them to me."

"Thanks for filling me in. I meant to ask you sooner. I really have been on a mission these past few weeks and—" I'm making excuses. "I'm sorry I didn't ask you myself."

He just smiles at me. "You know that and meeting the baby have got me thinking of moving back here so I can be closer to you and Hope. Funny how such a little person can have a profound effect on a person's outlook and sense of…I'm not sure what to call it. It's not duty. I guess it may be hope."

Although the baby was quiet and slept most of the day, the night time is a different story. She cries and feeds constantly. There is so much spit-up; it is hard to say how much of the medicines she is getting. I will need to discuss this with her doctors tomorrow.

As the night wears on, my brother tells me to go to sleep, and he will take the first watch.

My brother is groggy. He's been up all night. He is holding the baby and rocking and even singing sweetly. It's very touching.

"I thought you were going to take half the night and wake me for the other half?"

"Oh, well, I guess I lost track of time. Of course, how often will I have this chance, to stay up all night with a lady?" He laughs softly.

"Oh, I see. She is irresistible, isn't she?" Amused, I softly pat her feet.

"Are you in love, little sister? I think you're in love. And I think I am in love for you, or maybe just the same as you."

"Yes, we are."

He utters, "I want to give you a gift. I want to give her a gift. Children don't reject. Children don't reject love." He sounds sleepy. "Not like us adults. We can reject and set up barriers and defenses. You know?"

"Hmmm?"

"I want to give her life and a chance at life."

I realize he is trying to tell me something, and I have no idea where this is going.

"She somehow reminds me of him. I have had great sorrow and guilt for still being alive. I bet someday she will also have guilt for being alive. Yes, I have guilt for being alive and for never contracting HIV. I think Angelo also felt some guilt for my staying with him." He nods as if in understanding,

"Maybe he felt he was prolonging my misery. But, if I could have, I would have switched places with him. If I could have, I would have given him my immunity. I thrived and he didn't." He sounds a bit dazed, but continues, "I want to share that. I think I could give her life, you know? It would mean something."

"So you are moving back to town?" I think I am following him.

"No, not just that. And I am not sure I am moving back yet. I am talking about my blood. My blood rejects HIV, and a baby won't reject blood, won't reject stem cells. A baby won't even reject mismatched stem cells. Babies don't reject! You see where I am going? Do you see my proposal?"

"You look tired."

"No, I am serious. There's that story of the guy who cured his HIV by a bone marrow transplant from a person like me, a person who rejects HIV."

"Oh, who's the cute, overthinking geek now?" I laugh. "All these years picking on me for my zany ideas, and you, you are just like me."

"No, this could work, and you have a donor all set up. Me." He looks less tired, as if a switch turns on and he ignites. "We should do this; we have to do this!"

I have more sleep than he does, and I am starting to realize his plan. "Do you think it will work?"

"I think we should try. I think this is meant to be. We have to try. And these medicines...I don't know. I guess we can do this for years and years, but think about not having to." He looks exasperated. "I can't really say how much medicine she even got. I mean, there was so much spit-up. I think she has worn every baby outfit you have. I even did laundry, and when I ran out of burp cloths, I used kitchen towels, hand towels, whatever I could find."

I am feeling a bit guilty for sleeping.

He continues, "I am on my third load of washing. I can't say that this is not normal, but I have to believe that it is not normal. Then it hit me. It hit me!"

He is truly wired, and I am astonished I slept through three loads of laundry.

"Maybe we don't have to do this, all of this medicine, which I can't even say she is getting!" He softens and pleads, "Don't you see the plan? I can help her."

"But how? Has this ever been done?" My thoughts shift. I feel drawn to the baby, as I always have; is this part of the plan?

"I don't know? How close are you to the baby's doctors? Would they be able to help you?"

"I doubt it. Her doctors are pediatricians and infectious disease doctors, and we are talking about a stem cell transplant. Also, even though her initial HIV tests were positive, they plan to retest her at six weeks."

"You mean she might not have HIV?" He looks very puzzled.

"She definitely had the virus at forty-eight hours and at fourteen days, but they want to follow once more. I guess there have been very few false positives early in life, but I should not get my hopes up, because they are very rare."

"How rare?"

"Rare enough. I think that if we didn't live in a litigious society, they wouldn't bother to retest."

"We should be prepared. Let's get on the Internet; surely there's a group out there that can help us!"

I am not sure about this. "If I am a foster mom, can I make such a medical decision? I mean, for something experimental?"

"That's another question we will have to approach." He is quite determined.

"Can we use your laptop? I am not sure I should put this search on my computer." I am thinking about the militant social worker who will come to check in on me.

"I am not sure what that means, but, yeah, let's use my laptop."

The baby is asleep, and my brother is soon asleep as well.

Blog, people for stem cell research:

I need help. I really need some help. [I hope this is the right blog for stem cell transplant questions.]

I do not want to give my name or too many details, just an outline of where I am and why I need help for my infant daughter.

[I may ramble a bit, but no names, no places, and no times will be given.]

She has HIV. She was born with HIV. You may think that not many babies are born with HIV these days. There are so many treatments, and the rate of vertical transmission has dropped significantly, but sometimes it all fails.

[If you do not understand vertical transmission, you likely cannot help me.]

I don't have HIV. She is adopted.

A complicated process, from the hospital to home...

She is my [foster] **daughter.**

Does anyone know of any stem cell therapy being done for children with HIV?

[What harm is there in asking?]

It turns out that the blog is for anyone with any problem, and the responses are quite varied.

The first response is from an angry mom:

Don't hold your breath. My child has a brain injury from birth known as HIE. Don't ask me to explain too much or even what that stands for. Basically his brain was injured from lack of oxygen at birth. I couldn't get him into the trial for stem cell treatment. It is very, very limited.

In your case, you might try contacting companies who store stem cells, especially the for-profit companies who are always looking for publicity. That's what I am doing, and I am hopeful that they will help me get my son into a trial.

I respond with a simple:

Thanks for the advice.

In reality, this is not helpful, as I already have a donor, and my daughter will need very specific stem cells that lack the CCR5 receptor.

The next six responses are just angry posts questioning why can't they fix this or why can't they fix that or why do they even restrict stem cells? No doubt these are written by loved ones who are angry and desperate watching a loved one suffer with what mostly represents dementia of one sort or another, Alzheimer's, Parkinson's, and frontotemporal dementia.

Then there are a slew of quacks.

Hello, I am a doctor in [name of a foreign country]. I used to be associated with [name of a foreign medical institution of which I have never heard], but due to the controversial nature of my scientific experiments and certain regulations which limited my work, I have left such limiting institution.

Some then give a web address to click for more information. Some list conditions for which they have had "successful" stem cell treatments, including Alzheimer's, Parkinson's, frontotemporal dementia, HIE, diabetes, sickle cell disease, and on and on.

The diseases seem tailored to the group.

Some state that they can use any type of stem cell, including fetal or um-bilical or even self-derived.

Some ask that you e-mail to receive a quote; others state the cost is twenty to fifty thousand dollars up front, plus the cost of travel. One such business is on a barge off the coast of a foreign country, which allows them to escape certain regulations. Their cost is forty thousand dollars up front, but they will help with travel, visas, and transportation to their floating hospital. This par-ticular medical barge has links to a website and a PDF brochure.

I cringe to think that people actually would buy into such a setup. Is there really a hospital barge off of a foreign land? Or do they just get your money up front and then you never hear from them again? Or do you go to some foreign land to await a boat to take you to the hospital barge, but the boat never comes? Is this possibly smoke and mirrors? Like those fake scalpel-less surgeries where they fake the removal of the tumor by sleight of hand while actually removing chicken guts from your belly. Or could there really be a medical barge where you really do get some sort of concierge service to get you there, but you don't really get stem cells? Or do you really get stem cells, but who knows where they come from? Maybe there's a coexisting abortion clinic on the same barge. I can't help wonder what kind of generator powers such a facility. I guess the same kind that would power electricity on any ship. How sterile could it be? How could they run the appropriate lab tests? It just doesn't seem possible, but not impossible either.

I realize my brain has gone on a long tangent, picturing some mad doctor who lives on an old, dirty barge where he runs two simultaneous clinics. On one end of the barge, he does an abortion, and then he turns around to the other side of the barge, where he injects stem cells from the abortion into some awaiting victim. Sounds like the beginning of an interesting horror flick, or medical nightmare.

Unbelievably the person who is caring for someone with frontotemporal dementia asks if they have ever treated anyone with the diagnosis. He/she gets the same brochure link response and is encouraged to e-mail or call for more information.

I wish I could see what kind of information the person receives.

Several other bloggers issue warnings.

Don't fall victim to this quackery. They will take your money and maybe even take you for a ride, but you won't be cured.

We should be able to ban this kind of solicitous cr@p from our website.

Only decent and real information please!!!

Don't give money for false stem cells.

Some responses follow with a blog rumor of a person who went to some foreign land and had some amazing recovery. Even though he/she had to scrape together thirty thousand dollars with the help of family and friends, it was totally worth it. Your health is worth it!

These are followed by blog rumors of people who got scammed.

Don't believe these scammers who say they know someone who was cured. That's BS!!! People who write this BS just work for those overseas scammers!

Amazingly, in just a few hours, there are several screens of responses, what would amount to several pages of comments. None of the comments are of any worth to me. I am realizing how futile this blog is—really just a bunch of junk! What a sad and futile waste of my time!

The doorbell rings and I jump. I click on a safe search site, and then I delete my web history. I close the laptop and go to answer the door.

My parents enter with bagels and coffee.

"How did the night go?" My mom barges in. "Oh, that is too cute!" She squeals at my brother sacked out on the couch with the baby on his chest. Then she speaks in a whisper, hoping not to awaken them. "I should really get a picture of that." She giggles softly. She pulls out her phone and snaps a photo.

She walks closer to the couch and inspects the burp cloths and towels; she wrinkles her nose. "Where is your laundry basket?" she whispers.

I just go get it, but it's partially full of clothes. I inspect the dryer and put more clothes into the basket. I quickly take the basket to my bedroom and toss the clothes on the bed to fold. Then I return with the laundry basket.

My mom starts throwing all of the clothes and wipes into the basket. There is quite a bit, considering it has only been one night. The yellow-white stains smell of rotten milk, sort of sweet and sour; they're on everything she puts into the basket.

I follow her to the washing machine. Still in a whisper, she says, "This is a lot of spit up. Do you think you need to try a different brand of formula?"

"I am planning to call the pediatrician today."

She nods in approval. "Is this hypoallergenic soap?"

I nod.

"I guess that's good for the baby, but we will have to see how everything smells afterward. If it's still cheesy smelling, we can rewash it all."

There is a load in the washer that needs to be moved to the dryer. My mom smells the clothing as she moves them to the dryer. The clothing smell seems to meet her approval. She fills the washer, and both machines go to work. My mom must have seen me dump the clothes in my bedroom, because she goes straight into my room to the pile and starts to fold.

"We can get these folded while your dad sets up breakfast."

We are quick at folding together. Some of the outfits elicit "aw"s and "how cute" or "simply adorable" comments. Occasionally she gives one a sniff and shakes her head and puts it into a pile to go back into the wash. When we are done, that small pile goes right in with the current load. Then she asks me where to put the clean clothes.

I open the closet and point to the mostly empty shelf. I notice the bassinette. Oops!

"Okay, you will need a chest of drawers. I think I already have that on my list." She places the clothing in piles on the shelf. "I didn't realize you had a bassinette," she says, bending down to inspect the little bed. "Where did you get this?"

I am surprised she did not follow that with the suggestion of a secondhand shop or something to that effect. I collect myself and remind myself I must tell the truth but not give too much information. "As you know, Hope's mom died, but she had a few items for the baby."

"How did you get those items?"

"I picked them up." I try to sound like it is a standard procedure.

My mom looks at me, and I know she has many questions, but she changes the topic. "Well, let's get some breakfast; it could be a long day!"

My dad has put breakfast on the table, meaning that there is a brown paper bag and a brown carton with coffee on the table where he is sitting, reading the paper. My mom sighs loudly when she sees this. Then she puts out some dishes in a noisy fashion. She opens the bag with much rustling.

To which my dad replies, "I didn't want the coffee or bagels to get cold."

"Well, would you mind getting some coffee cups, milk, spoons, and knives?"

"I think there are some plastic utensils." My dad starts pointing to the bag, but then just goes to the kitchen for the items requested.

My mom opens the cream cheeses, one honey and one chive. "We bought two everything bagels, one plain, two cinnamon raisin, and one jalapeño cheddar bagel. Which would you like, dear?"

I smile. She knows and hands me the jalapeño cheddar. She says, "I really can't see how you can eat that, especially while drinking coffee."

My dad says, "I'll have an everything."

My mom hands him one, but asks that he please pour three coffees.

We load up the cream cheese, pour milk in our coffees, and eat silently for a brief while.

My mom cannot handle silence. I know this, and I am trying to think of something to say, but it's too late.

"So, honey," she starts in, "what other items did you pick up that were Hope's mom's?"

"Not too much; a few outfits, some diapers, and a bassinette."

"Did you go to where she lived?"

"No."

"No?" she counters.

"No." I take a big bite.

"Then how did you get the items?"

I chew for a while. I eventually speak. "I had hired a private detective who went to her place." I know that now I will get questions regarding the PI.

"Oh, so he got the items?"

"He was a big helper." I take another bite.

"So why did you hire a PI?" She asks the anticipated question.

I eventually swallow and then take a swig of coffee and swallow as well. "My lawyer said that if I was to think about adopting, that I might want to hire a private detective first to make sure that there weren't any family members who might surface and want the baby." I say nonchalantly.

"And there aren't any, right?" My mom is very focused, as is my dad.

"Right," I confirm.

"Well, what else do you know about the mom? What else did the private investigator find?"

"Not a lot; both of her parents are deceased. She was a college student without many resources."

"Did he try to find the father?"

"Yes, but he didn't locate any possibilities."

"None, how is that possible?" My mom is disbelieving.

"Well, she was a college student. I think she was young and maybe foolhearted."

"And by foolhearted, you mean loose."

My dad gives my mom a warning glance.

"Hope is innocent," I reply.

"So there's no daddy that the private investigator could find?" she clarifies.

"No." I pick off a jalapeño and pop it in my mouth, to which my mom makes a face.

My dad finally pipes in, "Your brother looks sacked out. How did the night go?"

"Hope was pretty fussy at night. I guess she has her days and nights mixed up." I think I've heard that expression before.

"You don't seem too tired, but I guess you are used to being up all night, huh?" my mom assumes.

"Actually, he was just supposed to take the first four hours, but he never woke me up," I admit.

"Aw, he is such a sweet brother!" My mom beams.

"He is," I agree.

We finish breakfast, and I clear the plates. My dad retracts behind the newsprint, and my mom takes out a notebook.

"Now that we have a moment, tell me what you like to eat, and I'll make a list and send your dad for groceries."

"I suppose just make foods that can be divided up and freeze well."

"Like lasagna," my mom replies.

Not my favorite, but I know that doesn't really matter. My mom is already listing the ingredients of lasagna.

"And stroganoff, and fiesta casserole." She continues to scribble. "Now what would we like for lunch and dinner? How about sandwiches for lunch? I'll add rolls and sliced turkey and Swiss to the list, and then what is for dinner?"

"How about we have fiesta casserole for dinner?" my dad requests. "You can make a large amount and then freeze the leftovers."

"Um-hm," my mom responds suspiciously. "Well, okay." She finishes the list and then slides it across the table to him.

"All right, honey, just let me finish my coffee."

I take a moment to call the infectious disease specialist. I go into my bed-room as I call. They tell me to try mixing the medicines together in one bottle and give in small amounts with each feeding, followed by a bottle without the medicines. Or I can try giving her the medicines with a dropper and then followed after a bit with the formula. No, they don't need to see her sooner, just do my best. If neither of those works, then at the next visit let them know, and they can try adding a gastrointestinal agent. "Okay," I think, "that was not too helpful."

My mom is anxious to hear what they told me. I tell her they told me to give her time, to give her smaller amounts with breaks in between because she is still very young.

"But what if that doesn't work? Did you tell them how much laundry you have done?"

"They said if this doesn't work to call back, and they could add some gas-trointestinal agent."

"What does that mean?" my mom argues.

"It means we will try smaller amounts." I smile brightly.

My dad is out and my brother and the baby are asleep, which leaves my mom and I alone to talk.

"Mom, do you mind if I step outside and go for a short walk? I could use some air."

"Would you mind if I came with you?" she says unexpectedly.

"No, please come along," I encourage.

"But what if your brother wakes up and he wonders where everyone is?"

"Oh yeah, that's true. We could leave him a note," I suggest.

"No, no, you go; I'll just read the paper for a while."

"Oh, all right, and you can go when I get back—if you want."

She flings her hands as if to say "Off with you; don't worry about me."

I step outside, and it is a crisp day. Cool, but sunny. The air just feels good. I walk for about twenty minutes, just long enough to clear my head, but not too long to seem to be avoiding my family, or Mom.

When I return, my mom is reading the paper and offers a pile for me to read as well. When she reads, the paper is down on the table so she is not covered.

After a while, she looks up. "Is it okay if I ask you about Hope's mom?"

This is unusually considerate of my mom. I figure my brother must have coached her. I am very, very tempted to say no, just to see if she can really abstain from inquiry. I know it's of no use. "What do you want to know?"

"Well, how did she die?"

"She died of pneumonia."

"Is that common? I mean is that all?"

"No, it's not common, but it does occasionally happen. Just like occasionally a college kid will get meningitis and die. It's not common, but it happens."

"Oh, so that's it." She eyes me cautiously.

I take her reply as a comment instead of a question, and I choose not to answer.

After a brief pause, she continues, "So what happens to someone like that after they die? I mean, does the state have a group burial?"

I'd like to say, "Beats me," but I cannot. "In this case, I claimed the remains."

My mom is taken aback. "What? What did you do with them?"

"They are in that box on the bookshelf; she was cremated."

"What?" My mom is still trying to pull this all together. "Why did you have her cremated? Why do you have the remains?"

"She was cremated before I claimed them." I realize I am getting into sticky territory, because I didn't have her cremated, and I don't want to explain too much. "She had an autopsy, and I don't know how she came to be cremated. Anyway, no one wanted her remains, and I thought maybe Hope might someday want them or at least want to know where she is."

"So you took the remains?" She is shaking her head in disbelief. "Why not just keep a photo? Did she have any photos with her belongings?

"No, none that I was privy to," I say, thinking a photo might have been nice.

"Do you think that they routinely cremate after an autopsy, or only after a certain time passes if no one claims the body? Where did you get her remains?"

I try to look as puzzled as my mom. "You know, I was going through legal paperwork and meetings and a two-day parenting course, when my lawyer said that things were looking favorable for me to fost-adopt the baby. Then he recommended that I get a private investigator, as I told you before. The private investigator did most of his investigating without me, which is the norm, I am guessing, as this is the first private investigator I have ever hired. Anyway, like I said, I was busy with—well, you can't imagine all that I have done in the past few weeks. He helped me to obtain these items, which I didn't have to take, but I did some reading, and I thought it might be nice for Hope to have some objects from her real mom to help her make some connection. I guess I read that adopted children often want to know about their biological parents."

My mom is just shaking her head in amazement. Then she gets up and goes to the living room and points to the box.

I just nod.

She comes back to the table. "Well, that is quite a story."

I sense that the phone lines will be burning between my mom and her friends tonight.

About noon the baby awakens and so does her bed. I am ready with a pre-made bottle, which she greedily gulps down, still in my brother's arms.

My dad has arrived with the groceries, which he and my mother sort out in the kitchen.

My brother whispers to me as he slings a small towel over his shoulder and readies the baby to burp, "No medicine, right?"

I nod, amazed that he has become adept at child care overnight.

"How long was I out?"

"Not too long. We are about to start making lunch."

He pats the baby's back and yawns at the same time. The baby seems content for a while and rests her head on his shoulder. "Did you change the laundry to the dryer?"

"Yes."

My mom comes to evaluate the scene. She makes lots of baby faces and baby talk. "Who made lots of pukie last night?" She tickles Hope's toes. "Who made pukie?" Hope starts to cry. "Oh, don't cry, darling, don't cry. Let Grandma hold you so your uncle can get cleaned up."

Grandma is holding Hope, and my brother goes to shower, and I make sandwiches in the kitchen with my dad. My brother calls out to ask for some soap, which I am certain is in that bathroom, but then I realize he just wants to ask me about the vomit and whether I had a chance to talk to the doctors. I relay the morning events to him. We both agree that Hope has done well with the first medicine-free formula.

I ask him about dirty diapers, as that is the best way to tell what a baby is taking in, and he reports, "Three wet and one dirty, really stinky diaper that I had to set outside in the trash. I couldn't leave that in the house. Maybe we should look into a diaper trash keeper of some sort."

"I'll get it on mom's list!"

The week goes by quickly. My parents return to the baby megamart to buy a diaper trash keeper that is quickly put at the top of the list. She and

146

my dad also buy a glider, and my mom arranges for three of her friends, the three who will also host my baby shower, to buy a chest of drawers with a changing table on top. The two larger items are soon delivered and set up. We also set out the bassinette, which is an easy way to keep Hope nearby.

Hope is crying from her bassinette, to which my brother responds, "Coming my little angel, little Ms. Hope Angela!"

"Hope Angela. Is that her name?" my mom asks.

"Yes, it's nice, don't you think?" he responds.

Mom eyes us both as she thinks about this. Again, I feel she is going to ask us about the secret we are keeping. She looks a little uncertain, but she eventually agrees, "Yes, Hope Angela is nice."

Hope is a lot of work, and she seems to have most of her problems with crankiness and vomiting at night. My brother is still thinking about his proposal and how we can make it work. I tell him about my blogging adventure and what a waste of time that seemed to be. He still does research on the computer at night, but there's not much good information. He might know someone in the medical field who can point us in the right direction.

I have to take the baby to doctors' appointments, which I tell my mom is just because Hope was born prematurely, and they want to make sure she's growing well and eating well. I put emphasis on eating. Hope does still vomit a bit, and so I don't need to explain any further.

We see the infectious disease (ID) specialist, and a few days later, the pediatrician. I tell the pediatrician that the ID requests that he draw some blood work on Hope. I also report the spit-up and ask about a gastrointestinal agent. He says he could prescribe a promotility agent, like Reglan, but he's worried about side effects. He just encourages smaller and more frequent feedings.

The next day a nurse calls to tell me Hope's a little anemic and all of her counts are a little low. Hope will need another blood draw in two days, and the nurse confirms an appointment.

Blog, people for stem cell research:

That day Hope vomits with some blood streaking. I call back to her doctor, who prescribes the anti-ulcer agent, Zantac. We barely get one dose of Zantac into Hope, when later that evening there's more blood in her vomit. I get a moist towel and wipe Hope's face with concern. Hope wrinkles her little brow and then gurgles up bright red blood, and we all rush her to the emergency room.

As I carry Hope back to the hospital, I feel the world is moving very slowly around me. She has blood streaked on the front of her clothes. Attendants rush to us to get us into a room. I know this is all happening, but I feel like I am barely a part of it; they are moving, and I am stuck, nearly frozen.

I feel myself sinking back to a place in the world without meaning, where I go along with my daily routine, chores, and jobs, feeling numb, just another nameless story of loss. Any plans or ideas I attempt seem futile.

PART II

THE BROTHER COUNSELOR

Screening

I am sitting in a small room, like a broom closet, looking at a computer screen.

"Click here to begin your questions."

"Are you over eighteen years of age?"—Yes

"Are you in good health?"—Yes

"Have you had a fever in the last week?"—No

"Have you had any flu-like symptoms in the last week?"—No

"Have you ever had cancer?"—No

"Do you have any tattoos?"—No

"Have you traveled outside of the country in the last three years?"—No

"Have you traveled to any of the countries on the given list in the last five years?"—No

"Have you spent more than two weeks on a farm in Europe in the last five years?"—No

"Did you ever receive a blood transfusion before 1980?"—No

"Were you or are you in the military?"—No

"Did you ever receive the smallpox vaccine?"

—No

"Do you live with someone who has had the smallpox vaccine?"—No

"Have you ever had hepatitis?"—No

"HIV?"—No

"Chagas' Disease?"—No [Huh?]

"Babesiosis?"—No [Huh?]

"Have you ever used drugs?"—No

"Have you ever traded sex for drugs?"—No

"If you are a woman, are you pregnant?"—NA

"If you are a man, have you ever had sex with another man?"

[Pause]

I am not sure what to think.

[Stunned]

I sigh. Angelo is here in the hospital, and none of his medicines seem to agree with him. He stopped the last regimen because of elevated liver enzymes; now he's back in the hospital with low blood counts.

Bruising all over his body—that was our first clue.

On admission, a nurse obtained Angelo's consent for a blood transfusion. She inquired about any designated blood units. Angelo and I both looked stupefied. She clarified and asked if anyone had donated blood specifically for Angelo's sake. He said, "No." Neither of us had ever heard of donating blood for a designated recipient. I felt the stare of the nurse saying, "Why haven't you donated and designated blood for him?" I felt Angelo's eyes saying, "It's no big deal; don't worry about it."

Maybe I am too sensitive and I over thought the situation, but I felt certain in that pause before signing that both he and the nurse gave me looks.

Giving blood seemed like such a simple thing that I could do for him. Why hadn't I thought of it before? I'll just go to the blood bank, while he is resting, and donate blood specifically designated for him. Easy enough, or so I thought.

So here I sit, looking at the computer screen, in a bit of a quagmire? Was I stupid, or perhaps naive to think that I could just donate blood?

I sigh, not knowing what to do. I can't lie and say no, especially in the situation for who the blood will be donated.

But if I click yes, then my session will be terminated, right?

I am certain that if I click yes, that a screen will appear that says something to the effect of, "Thank you for your time, but we are not able to accept your blood."

[Pause]

I almost want to click yes, just to be sure, but why? I know the answer—my session is over. I click the little icon at the bottom of the screen that says "return to main page," and I walk out. I do not bother telling anyone; I am not sure why. Could it be shame? I don't know, but I just keep walking, and I don't stop until I'm back at the bedside of Angelo, who is quietly sleeping. I whisper, "I'm sorry."

I am *still* sorry.

This memory ambushes me as I sit in the ER waiting room.

Déjà vu in a sense, and only now am I reminded that I am never supposed to give blood. I have had sex with a man, a man who died with HIV.

Dad finds a newspaper while mom talks away. One minute, it's, "Oh, poor Hope, the poor little dear." In another minute, it's, "She never should have taken on such a child! I don't think she knew what she was getting into." A moment later, it's, "Well, what good was that gastrointestinal medicine anyway? The medicine was for acid reflux or ulcers. How can they prescribe something without looking into what the problem is? I mean, maybe it's reflux or an ulcer, but what if it's not? Maybe it's a parasite! You don't think that Hope could have some sort of parasite do you? Or maybe it's some other sort of infection? Hope's mom died of some pneumonia; do you think that Hope got it too?"

But Angelo has been dead almost four years. And before that, as his illness was progressing and he was becoming the ghost of himself, we had not had sex, likely in the two years prior. So, no sex with another man for six years, I think, though I will admit the end was a bit of a blur. Is six years long enough? Is it long enough to claim that I am clean?

Then she goes into rumors. "I heard of this adoption where the real mom was doing all kinds of drugs, and the kid was damaged goods from the start. The poor adopting parents never really got the full scoop on the baby until they somehow, I can't remember how, found out, and then they tried to reverse the adoption. Well, it took a lawyer to help them. They were only allowed to reverse the adoption after threatening to sue the adoption agency."

How could I have thought about donating stem cells to Hope? How could I possibly face the screening?

Then there's a story of some missed diagnosis of a food allergy or a digestive enzyme deficiency, and another story that I give up on trying to follow. Actually maybe it was the same story, something about a baby with high fat content and liver failure. I am beginning to see the genius of my dad's newspaper trick. Then she goes into a tirade about adopted babies can be cute, and sometimes they don't cause any problems when they're young, but then they grow up to have all sorts of problems. "Remember the 'so-and-so kid' who grew up to be such a drug addict? I can't tell you the worry that child caused his parents, not to mention the thousands of dollars they kept spending on rehab, all wasted. Oh, and remember 'the so-and-so kid' who kept running away, and all the things he stole? Took his parents' credit card and spent well over ten thousand dollars one time running away, and on another occasion he stole his parents' jewelry and pawned off all kinds of things, including his father's Rolex."

If I re-face such screening, what or how will I answer? If the situation comes up, I feel like I should try. I could take the questions to mean in a certain amount of time, say in the last five years. Furthermore, I've never done drugs. I've never had hepatitis. I've never had a tattoo. I've never traded sex for drugs or money. I've been tested for all kinds of diseases, and I don't have any. I just fell in love with a man, who is now gone.

"Is it just the prematurity, or do you think that Hope's deformed? I mean, maybe she has some problem with her esophagus or stomach or something?"

I am a bit lost in my own thoughts, but I manage to shrug. I am glad my sister is not here.

"Do you think that Hope could have swallowed some foreign object? But what could she have swallowed? It's not like she's a toddler who is getting into trouble."

I am very tempted to tell my mom the truth about Hope, the whole story, if for no other reason than to get her to stop talking for a while. Tempting, but I can see why my sister doesn't want to share the birthmother's story. Then I imagine one of my mom's friends sitting in an ER waiting room, telling a story about this crazy doctor who knowingly adopted a baby with HIV and didn't tell her own parents, and can you imagine how the poor grandparents suffered, not knowing what was really wrong with the baby? I chuckle.

"What's so funny?" mom asks.

"Nothing, Mom. Why don't we just wait to see what's wrong, huh?" Miraculously my mom's rambling ceases. Her nervous chatter now gives way to a worried stare and wringing of her hands.

How can I possibly get past the screening? I don't know, but I think I may have to. She could die if I don't. She could fade away, just like Angelo. Something in me just knows this. I think, "Oh, Angelo, what should I do?"

I know it's meant to be.

It has to be.

About two hours later, my sister comes out to the waiting room. She tells us in a tired voice that Hope's blood counts are low. She looks directly at me and says, "We are not sure why."

My mom pipes in with the expected, "How did they miss this before she was discharged from the hospital? Shouldn't they have checked for this?"

"Hope is going to be admitted. Visiting hours are over, but if you want to see her before leaving the hospital for the night, then you can come with me for a few minutes."

We follow her to one of the ER areas. Hope looks so much more frail, weak, and pale. How did we not notice this before? She is in a clear plastic bassinette with a warming device overhead. She has an IV with a rather large unit of blood hanging, and I notice some bruising around the IV. She is only in a diaper and has a little silver-metallic heart sticker on her chest and a little beige band with a blinking red light on her foot. With each blink of the red light, Hope's foot trans-illuminates, glowingly red with darkened blood vessels. Both of these stickers have wires leading to a screen showing her heart rate and oxygen levels.

We all soften when we see her.

"Oh, you poor darling." My mom starts to cry. "You get better. We are all so worried about you." She reaches out and puts her hand on Hope's leg without the monitor. "You have to get better, okay?"

My dad just puts an arm around mom.

I look at my sister, who is quietly fighting back tears.

I fight back tears also.

Soon a transport team comes to move Hope to the ICU. My sister says she will see her settled in and then either sleep with Hope in the ICU or, if that's not allowed, find an on-call room in which to sleep.

I ask if she needs me to bring her anything, but she says, no, that the hospital is her second home, and she has supplies in a locker.

We solemnly say good-night and promise to return as soon as visiting hours begin in the morning.

I drive my parents back to my sister's home, where my parent's car is. My mom offers for me to stay with them for the night, and I politely decline.

My parents follow me inside to gather a few items. I am hoping they don't linger too long. My mom eyes the bloody rags by the couch and asks if she can help with anything. She starts moving toward them, and I block her way and respond, "Please don't worry about that; I'll get it cleaned up." I assure her, "Really, it's no trouble; I'll do a quick clean-up, then I am going to try to get some rest so that I can get back early in the morning."

My dad agrees. "We should all get some rest." He then gently guides my mom to the front door.

Mom nods and kisses me good-night. "We will meet you at the hospital tomorrow. Just call me on my cell if you need anything."

They leave, and the house is silent.

I get a trash bag, and I throw out the bloody items, including my shirt. My sister had placed an old, worn but soft throw blanket on the couch, which sadly also goes into the trash bag. Luckily for this, the couch was spared of any staining. I sort a few more of Hope's items and then do laundry. She had a notable amount of spit-up, and only now I notice a few milk stains have pink smears or brown flecks. I throw them into the machine and choose the cold cycle.

I wash up and get ready for bed. I am tired, but it's a melancholy tired, a defeated state that doesn't yield easily to sleep.

In my dreams Angelo is signing a consent form that is on a huge roll of paper, a never ending scroll that runs off of his hospital bed and onto the floor, fading into some unclear depth. He views a section regarding blood transfusion, and a nurse keeps pointing and instructing him to "Check here and sign here and initial here..."

I awaken with an idea.

I manage to wait until 7:00 a.m. to call my sister. Visiting hours begin at 8:30 a.m., and I want to see if she needs me to bring anything or make a run to the store for anything. She declines but offers for me to meet with her a little earlier for breakfast, which she states is also the only meal that the hospital reliably does well.

I meet her at the front of the cafeteria. Her hair is wet, and she is wearing scrubs supplied by the hospital. As we walk through the cafeteria, I realize that everyone at the hospital knows her. It's a bit like walking with a celebrity, I assume. Many ask about her daughter: "How is she doing?" They ask about my sister: "How are you doing?" They state, "We're praying for her," or "We are all thinking about you two," and so on.

The exchanges are brief; my sister makes replies such as, "She's doing okay," and "We are fine," and "Thank you." It's interesting to see how the medical community interacts—an occasional touch on the arm or the shoulder or a hug, there's a lot of feeling in their words though the words are brief. They seem to say, "We are busy and we know you are busy, but we are here for you if you need us."

We get trays, and I fill mine with eggs, French toast, and bacon. We sit in a semisecluded area meant for the hospital personnel. There are not many employees seated, though many come and go, again showing the buzz of the hospital; they sit and eat and chat briefly and continue on.

"So how is she?" I am anxious to hear about Hope.

"She looks much better after the transfusion," my sister says rather plainly, but her eyes show stress.

"How long do you think she will be in the hospital?"

"Actually they will watch her today; they are moving her to a regular room while we are eating. Her red cells and platelets dropped, but they have been replaced. Her white cells never fell, which is a blessing or she would be here a lot longer. So they plan to check her counts at four p.m., and if they are still okay, then she might be going home tomorrow."

"Really, that seems a bit quick, doesn't it?"

"We would need to bring her back every few days for blood counts and watch for any further bleeding."

"What caused her to bleed? Don't they need to check her stomach? What caused all of her vomiting? I'm guessing the medicines, so what are we supposed to do with that? And what happens if her counts drop again?" I don't mean to inundate her with questions, but sending Hope home without getting answers seems rather cavalier.

"Yeah, a pediatric gastroenterologist is supposed to see her today, but I got to speak to him on the phone last night, and he thinks he can just treat her with reflux medicines. She will stay off the antiretrovirals for a few days, maybe a few weeks, and once we know her blood counts are stable, we will try some new HIV medicines with close follow-up and monitoring. " She speaks flatly and then begins to eat.

Incredulous, I reply, "I can't believe it. I mean, don't they have to do more tests, check her bone marrow, or something?"

"No, not yet, not unless this all continues; it's a known reaction to treatment."

I want to ask her if she trusts the doctors here, but then I realize that might be insulting.

As we finish eating, Mom calls me on my cell phone. My sister mouths to tell her Hope is doing fine and out of ICU, no rush. Mom is surprised that I am already at the hospital; she is glad that things are going well, and if there's no hurry, then she and dad will come after lunch because dad is tired and still asleep. The call is thankfully brief.

While I'm finishing up with mom, my sister gets a text that Hope is in her new room.

The next day Hope is released from the hospital. Amazingly, Hope looks well, more color, pinker, and more alert. She gulps down formula, a new, gentle version with reflux medicines that we mix in.

My sister has done a remarkable job dealing with mom and all of her questions. Whenever mom poses a question of whether the doctors have thought of something or tested for something, my sister responds matter-of-factly in the "We have" format.

The next two to three days are uneventful. On day three, we take Hope to the infectious disease (ID) doctor for blood work. Her counts are dropping a little, but they're overall stable. We follow up in another three days; her counts are a little lower, so we will not restart her antiretrovirals yet.

Mom and dad visit a little less; mom is still actively planning the baby shower.

A few days later, Hope develops a cough and a mild fever. The ID doctor orders a direct admit for observation in the hospital.

Now her white counts have dropped, not to an emergent level, but enough to warrant a chest X-ray, pediogram, a spinal tap, and intravenous antibiotics. I was confused by the term pediogram until I realized that Hope is small enough to fit on one X-ray film to capture an image of her whole body.

She has been off antiretrovirals for almost two weeks. Her low blood counts could be a delayed reaction, HIV related, due to some other virus, or something altogether different. Eventually, the doctors draw out Hope's bone marrow, but they still have no answer.

Hope's admission seems unending; the hospital becomes her new home. Neatly graphed tests, blood draws and vital signs monitor her daily life.

Hope is now nine to ten weeks old. She has been in the hospital over four weeks. First she stayed in the pediatric ICU but then moved into a ward mostly filled with children unfortunate enough to have cancer. This particular ward is isolated, and the rooms have continual negative pressure, sucking air away, to help cut down infection. This ward is where Hope and my sister continue to stay. Some days Hope shows signs that she is getting better, other days worse: fevers up and down, cough better and worse, and white cells only making small changes. She had pneumonia, which is clearing slowly. Her chest X-rays still show residual evidence. Her little body has bruises and puncture marks mostly from medical procedures, but sometimes just the pressure from a diaper will cause a bruise on her tummy or thigh. Hope is sometimes cranky, but often lethargic, which is more worrisome.

My sister almost seems to distance herself, acting more like a concerned doctor than an emotional mom. She speaks in medical terms. I worry, but I am told to remember, Hope is still small, still fragile, and getting better may take some time.

Yes, I worry about Hope, but I also worry about my sister. I wonder if my sister is readying herself for the possible loss of Hope, as it seems that if Hope's white blood cells do not increase, in a matter of time she will get an infection that will kill her.

Every time Hope spikes a fever, every time there is a new finding on X-ray, every time there is a new lab test, we hold our breaths.

Her room area is flooded with gifts, mostly banners of sorts and balloons; flowers are not allowed in the unit, so any floral arrangements are given to the staff to take home. My sister and I take turns staying with Hope. My sister is living in the isolation room with Hope, but one night she comes home for a break.

She looks tired and worn. She's so good at hiding her feelings, the stress she must be feeling. At the hospital she maintains a wall of composure, but there are little telltale signs: the itchy scalp and the picked cuticles.

She confides in me that this is harder than she thought it would be.

"Regrets?" I ask.

"No, just…It's just that I feel like I can't get off of this emotional roller coaster. I feel like, life is just so hard sometimes, you know?" She looks almost broken.

"Of course I do."

"I know that I invited this emotional turmoil, but I couldn't prevent it either. I could just live my life alone, but that's not fulfilling. I mean, if I just lived alone, I could protect myself from this pain, but not really. Loneliness is just another form of pain; it's just duller. No, I think whatever happens, Hope and I are better off together, even if there is pain," then more reticently, "even if I lose her."

I think of the old adage, "It is better to have loved and lost, than to have never loved at all." But does she mean that Hope is dying? Does she know something that I don't know? "Is Hope dying?"

My sister threatens to break into tears, and musters, "I don't know. She is hanging on, but at anytime she could get an infection. She's on antibiotics, and they are working, but…"

I get up briefly and then hand her a tissue box.

She wipes her eyes and nose. She looks directly at me. "You know, I keep thinking about your proposal to give Hope your stem cells so she might have a chance not to have HIV. I keep hoping that the doctors will recommend a stem cell transplant, but I don't know if I should approach the subject or if I should just wait. I just didn't realize that she would be in the hospital for so long, and all of the tests. I am not even sure if they do stem cell transplants on children as young as Hope. I just don't know. What do you think?"

"About that...I need to talk to you about that." I collect my thoughts. "Have you ever given blood?"

"Yes."

"Then you know about the questions that they ask you before you donate blood, right?"

She nods.

"So, if you are a man, 'Have you ever had sex with another man?'"

Her face shows automatic realization of what I am telling her. "Oh, and HIV," she adds.

"Right, so I am not sure that I will pass screening."

"Oh, that changes everything." She looks down and then disconnectedly pleads, "Why do I bother?"

"But you are her mom, right?"

She nods, still looking down.

"So you can consent to what you think is in the best interest of your daughter, right?"

She looks perplexed. "Yes, but I can't make them."

"No, you can't make them do anything, but with your consent, I will try. I will try to be a stem cell donor."

"But you can't. I don't think that they will let you, and I don't have the authority to."

"No, but you have the authority to"—how to phrase this—"to consent for me to try. I mean, I could take the question to mean in the last five years and check 'no,' but I won't do it without your consent." My heart is pounding, and I am sweating.

She stares at me and blinks.

"I mean, I am clean. I have never used drugs. I have no tattoos. I have never taken or given sex for money. I don't have hepatitis or HIV. I need for you to believe that I am the right stem cell donor, even if the questions might not think it. I can help protect Hope. It's me, only me, and we may only get one chance. As her mom, you can make the decision, if you give me your consent."

She is staring at the floor, and her head is shaking. "I...Oh, God, I can't believe that I didn't think this all through. I don't know. I mean...to lie."

I nod. "I know, but I think it may be Hope's only chance. I guess it's bending the truth, and I wouldn't—well, I can't do it without your consent."

"Oh."

"I know that I am sort of making this your decision, your problem, but you have to understand that I can't do it any other way. I wouldn't do it any other way."

"Well, if you 'bend the truth' to pass screening, and they test your blood and you don't have any diseases, then your blood is probably her best option. I think then, as you say, that we have to try, because your blood is the only chance to give her natural protection."

"Please tell me you give me your consent to try."

"Yes, I do."

"I still can't guarantee that I can do this or that it will happen, but I know that if it comes up, then we have to try."

The doctors call a conference.

Three days after I get my sister's consent, she tells me that two doctors, the ID doctor and a pediatric hematologist, wish to hold a family conference to discuss Hope's progress, or lack of progress. They will meet us at 5:30 p.m. in family conference room 3A.

I plan a brief visit with my dad.

Going home envelopes me in warmth and gives me a strange sense of security. The smell of home really takes me back to my childhood. I am tempted to visit my old room, but I know the room has little resemblance to my childhood room; it has become the scrapbooking and craft center for my mom. At my last viewing, I could barely make out if there was still a bed inside the room. If I were to stay here, I would stay in my sister's old room, which has remained a bedroom, but now for guests.

I tell Dad that I need to borrow some clothes, as I didn't really pack for such an extended trip. My dad asks me how I am managing. I tell him all right, but he clarifies with asking how I am managing to take off so much time from work. I tell him that I had saved up some vacation, but that I am also taking some family leave time. He nods quizzically and tells me that when he was working, he took off only one day for each of his children's births—just two days total for "family leave time."

He does show me to his closet, where he takes out a few pants and shirts that look to be my size, and then invites me to try them on and take what I like.

I pick out a few jeans and plaid, flannel shirts. The jeans are super soft from years of wear. I swear I would buy Levi's if they all felt this way new. Heck, I might even buy Wranglers if they felt like this. The only unusual feel to them is the way the butt area sags. Thinking of Wrangler's, no, even if they were soft, the pockets are just too low. I have to cinch the jeans with a belt. Unfortunately my feet are bigger than my dad's or I would borrow some of his more worn-looking shoes as well. I hope my Choo shoes match all right. Looking in the mirror, I turn side to side, checking the continuity of the loafers with the jeans. The loafers are a bit pointy, but the orange suede does pick up some of the colors in the plaid; so, not seamless, but overall passable. Yes, this will do.

I fold up my clothes and grab another set of Dad's clothes and stack them together. I show my dad, and he nods with a jutting chin to show his approval. He gets me a plastic bag for my things and asks if I would like anything to drink or if I want to stay for a while.

My mom is out, and so he directs us to the refrigerator. He opens the door, not knowing exactly what drink choices might be available. I wouldn't say that my dad is a stranger to the kitchen, but my mom is the usual food and drink hostess. We open some Cokes and sit for a while at the kitchen table. He asks about Hope. He says that Mom is driving him crazy about the shower, and she needs to set a date. But when asked, my sister said to have it without her or Hope. We share a laugh.

Before leaving, I ask him to have Mom call me, and I will help plan her mischief.

The conference...

I arrive back at the hospital by 4:30 p.m. My sister notices my new attire and smiles with reassurance. We sit patiently near Hope and await our conference.

The ID doctor comes by Hope's room to take us to family conference room 3A. We follow him, but I know my sister knows where we are going. On the way he says the hematologist will join us shortly, but when we get to the room, he is already there.

The pediatric doctors don't wear white coats, as the bleached attire tends to frighten children. The hematologist is more immaculate, wearing a stiff-collared shirt, a tie with dogs on it, slacks, and well-shined shoes. He seems to take time to exact his look. His mannerisms are also more cautious, and he allows himself time to explain and think things through.

The ID doctor appears to be a less formal guy, with a half-tucked oxford shirt and a toy monkey attached to his stethoscope. He has no tie and wears penny loafers. His looks are efficient, as are his actions, and he is anxious to get started.

He begins, "By default, because Hope has a chronic infection, I act a lot like her pediatrician. I have seen blood counts drop with antiretroviral therapies, but they usually return shortly after stopping them. In this case, the medicines may have been the trigger, or maybe it was some other trigger. We have done testing, including two bone marrow biopsies, and we are just not sure why, but Hope's blood counts do not seem to be returning to normal. She has beaten a few infections already, but with low counts, her chance of a more severe, possibly life-threatening infection is very high. We do not wish to keep her in isolation, getting repetitive transfusions forever. I am sure you feel the same way." He stops to acknowledge our subtle nods. "So at this point we would like to approach the idea of a blood stem cell transplant. I have had a few children with HIV who have needed stem cell treatment, though mostly because of co-incidental cancer treatment. Hope doesn't have cancer, but we feel this is likely in her best interest." He pauses to cue the hematologist to join in.

On cue he says, "Stem cell transplants can be risky. Surprisingly, young children often do better than adults, but sometimes they can also have bad and unexpected outcomes. So we want to start this conversation, as finding the right donor can take time. During this time we will continue to monitor Hope's need for stem cells, and when we have everything together, by then if she has made no improvement, then we will likely proceed. Do you have any questions at this point?"

"What kind of time line are you looking at?" my sister asks promptly.

"I am guessing in the range of three to five weeks to line up a donor, so in the range of one to two months total. Hope will likely need to stay in the hospital during this time, but her prognosis could change. We are still hoping that her blood counts will recover; however, Hope's blood counts have shown no increase since her being admitted to the hospital. The more likely chance is that her blood counts will not recover, and so we should start this process." Evidently, this is the hematologist's show.

"As you know, I am a physician, and I have thought this over since Hope has been in the hospital with low blood counts," my sister asserts.

The other doctors nod.

"I am not really surprised by this possible recommendation. If at all possible, I would like my brother to be the stem cell donor, and I know he feels the same." She looks at me, and I am a little taken aback by her forthrightness.

The hematologist seems to look me up and down and then replies, "Well, we do normally look into family members, as they share genetics and are often better matches; however, given that Hope is adopted, there's no real necessity." He struggles to find the right words. "I mean, you can do it out of kindness, but it's very likely that we will find a better match from registries." He seems to give me a second look, and I am glad that I am in my dad's comfortable plaid, flannel shirt and jeans. Somehow, I feel protected. He continues, "There is a process, and it is also likely faster to match Hope's blood with one from donor registries."

"No, I don't consent to begin there," my sister says quite firmly.

The hematologist is very perplexed. "I'm sorry, but why?"

The ID doctor scratches his head and shifts awkwardly.

My sister gulps and then says, "I will tell you why." I am suddenly very nervous and tense. She goes on, "We happen to know that my brother's blood lacks the CCR5 receptor."

There is a moment of silence and notable appreciation on the other doctors' faces. Finally, the ID doctor inquires, "How do you know that?"

"He's been tested." My sister is short and abrupt.

"Why was he tested?" the ID doctor asks, needing clarity.

"He was in a study."

I can read that the ID doctor wants to ask why I was in a study. I can sense the two doctors' glares upon me, but neither asks why.

My sister offers, "He happens to know a doctor who studies this, and he also knows his results."

They sit stunned. They want to know more, I know, but they don't inquire further. The ID doctor just nods and says, "I see."

The hematologists blurts out, "He will—I am sorry. You will have to be screened. You will have to pass screening. Your chances are extremely minimal; I have to tell you that I think you are just wasting time."

I am not sure if I am supposed to feel threatened, but somehow, I do.

The ID doctor asks, "Are you a blood donor?"

"Uh, no," I look directly at him, and it feels as though we are both trying to read each other. I am tempted to explain more, but I go with the same short replies as exampled by my sister. Why, oh why did my sister bring up the CCR5 information?

"Okay." The ID doctor looks puzzled, as though he wants to understand what I know. I am sure he wonders if I ever had sex with an HIV-positive person and remained negative, because why else would I have been tested; or could I have just been part of a prevalence study, a random sampling of people to see how many lacked the CCR5 receptor. I am relieved to appreciate another possibility.

The hematologist breaks in. "Well, I will set you up with our stem cell donor coordinator. She will interview you and do a physical exam and blood work. Some of the blood tests take a while to return, so if we are starting fresh, then we will need to get started ASAP. I do want you to consider that you may be wasting precious time to see if you are a match, when we could just start the process form registries, which is where we will likely wind up anyway."

The ID doctor stumbles in. "Um, I am not saying that you will be the donor, but let's say that you become the donor, and if what you say is true and this could cure Hope, can we"—small pause to deliberate—"well, we would follow her, of course, but we might want to publish such a case. I mean, there is great, great interest in something like this. Would that be acceptable to you?"

Ah, that is why she told them. I am not sure if the question is directed at me or my sister, but we both look at each other and nod, then my sister says, "Yes, that would be expected."

The hematologist ponders aloud, "I have a question. It's a little awkward, though this conversation has been rather unexpected." He glances back and forth between my sister and me. "I understand that you adopted Hope, and you knew she had HIV. Did you know about your brother's blood and think of it with this possibility?"

My sister responds, "I am not sure what you are asking."

I can't agree more. I mean, we did think of it, but what is his point?

"Why did you adopt Hope, to begin with?"

"I did not adopt Hope thinking that I would cure her, if that's what you are asking. I have had infertility and then pregnancy losses and divorce, but I always wanted a child." She looks down as if experiencing some pain. "I have had emptiness, and then I saw Hope. I was randomly thrown into her life by assisting with her cesarean birth, and then her mother died, and there was no family who came to claim her. I felt something that I can't explain, but I wanted to be her mom." This pours out with evident angst.

"But you already had your brother picked out when we mentioned the stem cell treatment. How did you come to that decision?" he presses on with scrutiny.

"My brother came to the conclusion." She looks at me for added support.

Thank you very much for putting me on the spot. I understand that you are emotionally spilling your whole life, but I am not prepared for this. I transmit this with a brief glare in her direction. I realize that I better give an answer and quick. "Yes, I did come to the conclusion." I am wondering if I can stick to the short answer theme, but I know that won't work this time. I know exactly when the thought hit me: Hope vomited up her medicine for the umpteenth time, and I wished she didn't have to take the medicines and—eureka! I can't say it was then, it sounds too soon, so I say, "She doesn't seem to handle medicines well, and now she is here in the hospital several weeks with low counts, and I just realized a possibility."

"But there's nothing you did?" the hematologist interjects suggestively.

"Excuse me?" I retort.

"What are you saying?" my sister says at the same time.

The hematologist continues his questioning look, to which my sister responds, "If you think that we somehow made her counts go down in some way, which I can't think of any possible way, but no. Hope has been here several weeks, and what could I possibly be doing? No, if she were thriving on antiretrovirals like so many individuals with HIV are able to do, then we would all be happy for her to live a long life on antiretrovirals." She shakes her head incredulously.

I can't agree with her more, and yet, there's a part of me wondering if we wished for this in some way.

The ID doctor blurts, "No, no." And he looks at the hematologist. "That's a bit farfetched, don't you think?"

To this, he shrugs. "I know, but we've seen some very odd things before."

"No, I can't think of a way. I mean, unless she got some chemotherapy agent or radiation. No, no, I can't even imagine," the ID doctor retorts.

"Even for a physician?" the hematologist speculates.

"Risk her life? Are you kidding me?" my sister shouts.

The hematologist shakes his head, but finally concedes, "Okay, all right. I suppose there is no harm in ruling you out as a potential donor, other than a small waste of time. So I will have my coordinator call you." He looks at my sister. "I will give her your cell phone number; she should call you tomorrow morning, but if she doesn't"—he reaches into a coat pocket and withdraws a card from a silver case—"then call her tomorrow, say by ten a.m. We want to get started as soon as we can."

She takes the card and nods.

With this, he shakes her hand and mine and says he will keep in close contact. He opens the door and is the first to leave. The ID doctor extends his hand in a gesture to allow us to exit before him. We emerge and part our separate ways.

Afterward, Hope is moved to a slightly larger room in the isolation unit. This room has an imposing mirror, and I can't help but wonder if we are under some sort of surveillance.

Screening revisited

I meet the stem cell transplant coordinator the next morning. She is a tall woman with short, spiky, jet-black hair that shines in almost a blue hue. She has a rather angular jaw and wears dark red lipstick on her outer lips and black lipstick in the center. She has several piercings in both her ears and one each in her nose and lip, and when she begins to speak, I notice one in her mouth. Her name tag reads that she has a PhD. We are both wearing plaid, flannel shirts, but I am wearing khakis, and she is wearing a short plaid skirt that clashes horribly with her shirt. She has a red kerchief with a black skull print, plaid tights, and black army-type boots.

Silly me to think I'd be judged for my appearance. Somehow, I like her already, but I wonder if she has much contact with the children on the unit and what they might think of her scary Goth doll look. Also, how does she regard the uptight hematologist, and how does he regard her?

She directs me to a small examination room with an examination table and two chairs. She offers for me to sit in the side chair, while she sits in a similar chair facing a computer screen. She logs onto the computer and then gathers and types in my contact information. I notice her nails are bitten down to the skin. Then she gives me a five-page questionnaire to fill out that mainly goes over my medical history with subheadings of cardiac, cancer, pulmonary, psychiatric, endocrine, and so on. This takes some time, so she leaves the room to assist another. She periodically checks in on me, and when I tell her I am done, she returns to go over the form with me, typing away at the computer.

Once this is complete, she says, "Today will be rather short. I need to obtain your consent, and then I will draw some of your blood to see if you are a match. First, you will need to watch two videos. After the first one finishes, just open the door, and I will return." With this, she angles the computer screen toward me and clicks a "play" icon. Once the video starts and she ascertains that the volume and brightness are okay, she quietly leaves the room.

The first video is titled, "Becoming a Blood Stem Cell Donor," and begins with a doctor in a white lab coat who thanks me for my interest in becoming a blood stem cell donor. He states, "Without the help of people like you, thousands of sick individuals would die each year, as seventy percent of those in need of a stem cell donation do not have any suitable matching family member. First let's discuss what blood stem cells are."

With this, the doctor is replaced by a cartoon depiction of a person. "In our bones"—the person's bones become highlighted—"our marrow makes blood. The marrow is rich in blood stem cells." The picture focuses on a bone that becomes so enlarged that you can see the spongy texture of the bone and blood cells within its matrix. The blood cells are different colors: most are red, less are white and pink, and a few are blue. "Now let's talk about the kinds of blood cells in the marrow. The red cells carry oxygen to all areas of the body. The white blood cells fight off infection, and these pink guys represent platelets that help your blood to clot if you are cut." As each cell is brought out from the matrix, the corresponding name and function is given. "These rare blue cells represent stem cells, and you can see that there are much fewer of them. Stem cells can become or make any of the necessary blood cell types." With this, the blue cells become more blue cells, or they transform into red or white cells or platelets.

The doctor comes back on. "Sick patients may need stem cells to make blood for many reasons. Stem cells can be used to treat cancers, especially blood-borne cancers or leukemia, or to replenish blood in individuals who for various reasons are not able to produce the necessary or functioning cells that they need. Now let's talk about what you can do to donate blood stem cells." First he talks about joining a registry that can link you to any sick patient in the country. Next, he encourages a healthy lifestyle.

"What happens if you are a match? You will be contacted, and in many circumstances you can find out who the recipient will be and what disease he or she is facing. Please know that you are under no obligation to donate stem cells. Also, if you feel that you have not been keeping a healthy lifestyle or if you have been feeling sick, then you should likely not donate." He pauses and looks upward as if to show consideration. "Women who think that they may be pregnant are asked not to donate. Also know that you will not be charged any money for any of the testing or donation procedures. Furthermore, you will not be compensated in any way for the donation." He pauses with an unyielding stare.

"If you decide to donate, then you will be called for a complete physical, including a chest X-ray, EKG, and blood tests. These test results may take one to two weeks. The next step is finding out which method of blood stem cell retrieval will be used. The first method is called bone marrow aspiration." The cartoon person with the skeleton inside returns, and the focus turns to his hip. "During a surgery, under general anesthesia, a small hole is bored into the hip bone. Bone marrow is aspirated, or pulled out by syringe, and then prepared for the recipient." The cartoon person lies on an operating table, goes to sleep, and a syringe pulls up to his hip and sucks out some brown-red fluid. The fluid is magnified until the blue stem cells can be seen.

"The second way is called peripheral stem cell donation, or apheresis. In this case, you will receive injections over four to five days to help stimulate the blood stem cells and mobilize them into the blood stream." Now the cartoon figure is receiving a shot, and little blue dots multiply in his bones, mostly the hip bones, leg bones, and spine. These little blue dots then start to circulate through the arteries and veins, which also emerge on the screen. "Now we can retrieve the stem cells by drawing blood, filtering out the stem cells, and then returning the blood to the donor." The cartoon figure now has tubing from one arm, with red and blue dotted blood streaming out of him into a machine, where the blue dots are collected in a bag, and then only the red dots exit the machine and are returned to the cartoon man's other arm. "This procedure requires no anesthesia, but does take anywhere from three to six hours to complete the collection."

The narrating doctor returns and smiles at the camera. "Now that you know about stem cells and how you can become a donor, I thank you for your time and interest. I hope you decide to become a blood stem cell donor. Thousands of patients require blood stem cell donations, and you could be the match that saves one life."

The video is over, and I open the door.

The coordinator returns and asks if I have any questions.

I think of many questions, such as which method of retrieval will likely be used, and do the shots hurt, but I know that none of that matters unless I am a match. "What does it mean to be a match?"

"There are six proteins in your blood that we look at, and we try to match as many as possible between a donor and recipient; usually we need to match at least five. If less are matched, then there's much more risk of complications for the recipient." She answers as she pulls up a page on the computer for me to digitally sign and for her to digitally witness.

"What is the possibility of a match between two random people?"

"Slim," she acknowledges with a flat smile.

"Do they ever accept less than five matches?"

"In general, no, but sometimes there can be exceptions."

"Oh, that doesn't sound too hopeful." I puzzle it over. "I thought infants don't reject transplants because their immune systems are not yet mature."

"It's not the baby rejecting your cells; it's your cells rejecting the baby," she informs simply.

"I saw this documentary once about heart transplants in infants, where they didn't really match the donors and recipients because they showed that the infants don't reject the foreign tissue the way adults do." I have to ask even though I realize my questions may be bothersome.

"Yes, but the heart is an organ, whereas you would be donating blood stem cells with immune functions. Furthermore, babies can only accept hearts from other babies. I mean, you can't put an adult heart in an infant." She explains with a look that says, "Right?"

I can't say that I follow the difference. "So it all depends on whether I am a match for the recipient, and those chances are slim?"

She nods.

I know I have to try, and I check the box for digital signature.

"You could always wind up helping someone else," she encourages. "Are you ready for the second video?"

I nod, and she clicks, "play."

The second video is called "Jenny's Story." Jenny is a young lady whose sister has cancer and needs a blood stem cell donation. Jenny has her blood drawn, but sadly, she is not a match for her sister. The video states that although siblings are often matches, many times they are not. Jenny still joins the donor registry and is immediately matched to a young man with sickle cell disease in another state. Jenny asks herself, "Do I have what it takes to save a life, of someone I don't even know?" She looks at her sister, and they both exclaim, "Yes!" Jenny's sister also finds an unrelated donor among the registry. So while Jenny is going through the donation protocol, her sister is going through the recipient process. Jenny is in good health and passes the physical exam. "Wow, I've never had an EKG before. Is my heart okay, doctor?" I can see why they chose Jenny; she smiles through the whole process and looks youthful and energetic. She peripherally donates stem cells and needs daily injections given over four days to stimulate the stem cells in her blood. "The injections don't really hurt, but I did get some mild flu-like symptoms, a little bone pain, and an occasional headache," she says cheerfully.

For the day of the donation, they show her with an IV. We follow the blood from one of her arms, then through the tubing, then through the "continuous flow centrifuge," and finally back into her other arm. A narrator states that only two hundred milliliters of blood circulates outside the body at any time, which is a little more than half of a can of soda pop. Jenny pipes in happily, "I don't feel dizzy or faint." Then she's done and smiles some more. Her sister gets her stem cell transplant and looks invigorated. Jenny gets an e-mail from her recipient thanking her for her stem cell donation, which saved his life.

"Jenny's Story" sells an important message. I am certain that I am not the first person hoping to donate to a family member and, as stated, not all family members are matches. In my case, I am not even a family member, so my chances are "slim." This begs me to think about saving another, something I have not yet considered.

I open the door.

"Well, any questions?"

I shake my head, and again I have to check a box on the computer indicating I have watched the video. The coordinator checks the box as a witness.

Next, she prints out a consent form for stem cell donation in general and goes over this with me. The coordinator summarizes the form as she reads it aloud. "In consideration of becoming a blood stem cell donor, I am under no obligation to do so, I have no obligation to the recipient (whether known or unknown), and I am under no obligation to pay for anything, nor will I receive any compensation...Taking out stem cells does not injure a person or lessen their blood-making capacity...There are two methods of retrieving blood stem cells. If I am chosen and agree to donate stem cells, further consents will be necessary to go over the risks of the retrieval process...I have been given an opportunity to ask questions, and my questions have been answered in a sufficient manner."

Then she looks at me and asks, "Do you have any further questions?"

I have lots and lots of questions, but the answers can only be known with time. I shake my head and sign.

She is rather no-nonsense, and yet, somehow, I think she wants to help me. She takes my vital signs and draws some blood. She puts stickers on my blood and asks me to confirm that each sticker shows my name. "I will get this blood sent off, and if you are a good match, there will be further testing and such. I will be in touch." She says this as we exit the room; she doesn't say what happens if I am not a match.

As I am leaving, I see a sign on the entry wall saying that later in the day a stem cell donor will be holding a question and answer session for potential donors in the waiting area of this clinic. I note the time, 4:00 p.m., and I decide that if I am free, I will try to attend.

Screening amounted to much less than I thought. I leave feeling unsure and with a familiar naivety. I thought if I could get through the social questions all would be fine, but no, the biggest obstacle is chance. What's the chance that we match? Is it less than winning the lottery? "Slim," I hear her answer in my head.

I return to my sister in Hope's room.

"So, how did it go?" she eagerly asks.

"I think it went okay." She looks like she will burst if I don't tell her more, so I briefly and cautiously tell her it was all routine stuff, nothing that made me uncomfortable at all. I attempt to explain how everything hinges on whether I am a match. Screening determines compatibility, which is unlikely to favor me.

Then like me, maybe more so, she understands the uncertainty.

My leave from work is nearing its end. I have already had multiple calls from my office wanting to know when they can expect my return, which makes me a bit tense. I feel a commitment to Hope and my sister, and I will go through with our plan, all things willing.

My sister is thinking that I can move back here, and we can alternate working and taking care of Hope. This also makes me uneasy; I can stay with her for a while, but I know I need to return to my home and my job at some point. I love my sister and Hope. I could find a job here and a new home, but I know that I won't. With the circumstances, I don't want to seem like I am running away, and I am not, but this is not my home.

Hope has transfusions every few days. They hang a full bag of blood, drip in a small amount, and then discard the rest by dropping the remainder in a red trash bin. I almost wish they could save the remainder, maybe turning the drip on and off as needed, but as it reads on each bag, blood is perishable. If she only needed transfusions of red blood cells or platelets, then she could maybe leave the hospital, but because her white cells are low, she and my sister stay.

Surprise!

One day, to my sister's bewilderment, I enter the room with my laptop. My mom's friends are finally throwing her baby shower, and we are attending by webcast.

My mom takes up the screen. "Hi, sweetheart! Welcome to your baby shower! Look, I can see her! Look how surprised she is!" My mom seems just as surprised. "I actually was going to have the shower at the hospital, but your brother thought that might be a bit much, especially since Hope is still in isolation, and I didn't know if you would want to leave her side. So your brother thought it would be better if we just visited over the Internet. Surprise!"

My sister gets in front of the screen and says, "Wow, thank you both for planning the shower in this creative manner." She nods at me and mouths, "Thank you!"

My mom and her friends have already eaten their lunch, but my mom preserved one plate to show my sister the lunch menu. "Look, we had tea sandwiches with chicken salad, mixed fruit, and a side of asparagus." I am not sure what she is expecting my sister to say to that. Then she brings the cake to the computer and says, "Isn't this nice, honey? Look, a cake with little pink booties and pink icing that reads, 'Welcome Baby Hope.' Oh, isn't that nice!"

My sister nods and smiles at both food displays.

"Oh, I wish you were here to cut the cake. Anything you want to say to the ladies?"

"Um, thank you all. That all looks lovely. I hope you enjoy everything."

"Do you want me to save you some luncheon food?"

"No, that's all right. You all enjoy it."

"Well, of course I will save you some cake."

With that, the cake is cut and served, and my sister and I giggle at the women eating around the mounds of pink frosting.

After they have cake, my mom gets on the screen again. "Do you want me to save all the presents so you can open them, or do you want me to open them so you can personally say thank you to each guest?"

"Sure, you can open them." What else could my sister say?

So my mom sits and directs one of the ladies to take notes of who gave what, of course, so my sister can write thank-you notes, in addition to personally saying thank you via computer. Each woman brings my mom a gift and looks into the webcam and says something to my sister like, "Congratulations!" and "I hope she gets better soon!" and "I am so happy for you!"

Then my mom opens the card and reads it to my sister, then opens the gift and holds it up. The ladies all ooh and ah in unison. Then my mom or one of the ladies make a comment, such as, "Isn't that adorable!" or "Where ever did you find a pink leopard print onesie?" or "Don't you wish they made headbands like this for us?" as she tilts her head and holds the headband with a large fuchsia flower to her forehead.

My mom is really quite good at appreciating each and every gift and its gift bearer. My sister giggles at some of her comments but is gracious about each gift.

Overall, there are about twenty ladies and gifts. The presents seem to go on forever, but then suddenly they're done.

"Well, that's all of them! And of course we cannot forget our very gracious hosts and their gift. Remember, honey, the chest of drawers-slash-changing table?"

"Of course, Mom. We could barely get by without it! Thank you all, ladies, so much!" my sister replies.

The three hosts take up the screen and say, "You're welcome!" and "It was our pleasure!" and "Your mother is such a dear friend, and she has done so much for us over the years."

No doubt they owed her, and she orchestrated the shower that she was due.

There is a pause, and then my mom gets back on the computer. "Honey, do you think the ladies could see Hope? I was thinking that maybe they could get a view on the computer, if it wouldn't be too much to ask."

"Oh, of course," I say, and I direct the webcam toward Hope in her bassinette.

My mom circulates the laptop on her side, and one by one the women sigh and say, "How sweet!" and "The little angel!" and "Hello, precious!" and "Oh, bless her little soul!"

We sign off, and my sister gives me a hug and says, "Thank you for helping mom with that. The webcam was genius. Seriously, it was like a mini-shower, just hitting the highlights and with no chance of playing any stupid baby shower games!"

I give her a disappointed look; how could she want to miss even one second of something as special as that shower?

"No, really, thank you. That was perfect. Mom is happy, and I am happy!"

"It's good to see you happy!"

My next order of business is to expand my family leave to the full twelve weeks—even if it is without pay, which it most certainly will be. I have to talk with human resources and get paperwork to make sure that they will hold my job. I have worked for a large health maintenance company for several years, and legally, I believe they have to hold my position. HR asks me if I would like to apply for short-term disability, to which I answer no. Still, I go around and around regarding family leave versus short-term disability, alternating being on hold and speaking to managers of varying degrees. Finally: "We will have to get back to you on that one."

By conference call, the highest HR manager and I speak to the policy distributor about short-term disability. The distributor makes it clear that I am not disabled and therefore, I do not qualify. I could have told HR that. When there are no further questions on our end, the policy distributor disconnects. My HR manager then says, "There is family leave paperwork, but in general, people only take five to six weeks." Several hours later and multiple phone calls, I finally get them to resend the paperwork that clearly states that I can request up to twelve weeks off. Thank you, HR.

I fill out the form and I have the ID doctor sign it. I return the forms to HR without any response. When I call them, they can only tell me they are "considering my situation," after being on hold with no less than four different answerers.

My unit chair calls me to check in with me and basically reassures me that my job will be there, even if he has to rehire me. We joke about the irony in the terms Human Resources and Health Maintenance.

My sister considers going back to work, as she works shifts in this hospital where she and Hope have essentially moved in. It would seem to make sense. She could break up her monotony and earn some money. I could stay with Hope while she works, and she could easily check in on Hope while she works. She then considers the downsides. For one, it might not look right. Secondly, she would feel horrible if she were to miss something in regards to Hope's health. Finally and most importantly, she can't fully avoid seeing patients with infections in her work, and she couldn't risk bringing any infections back to the unit.

My sister fills out similar forms, twelve weeks—will that be enough time?

The ID doctor also signs her paperwork, and I have to admit that I have a small crush on him. Maybe I just hold ID doctors, like the one who treated Angelo, with the highest esteem, as they seem to exhibit beatific qualities. Too bad my new hero wears a wedding band.

The group session with a donor...

I tell my sister about the flier stating that a stem cell donor is going to hold a question and answer session, and I ask her if she would like to go.

She tells me that she would rather stay with Hope but that I should attend. I arrive as he is talking about the injections, and I gather that he donated by the peripheral method.

"The injections were no big deal, and I tolerated them quite well, until about the third night, when I noticed a deep burning back pain. Not severe enough to call the clinic or go to the hospital for, but enough that I was uncomfortable and unable to sleep. I was warned about bone pain, as the marrow in the bones is stimulated by the medicine. My arms and legs ached, almost like the prelude to catching the flu. I didn't want to take any medicine because I was afraid that when I donated the stem cells to my sister that she might have a reaction. I found that a hot shower really did the trick. For the next few nights, I slept in many layers and a heavy coat with the hood up, and then under all the covers. I did wake up kind of sweaty, and I was glad that my coat was easy to launder."

Some of the audience laughs.

"No, the injections aren't too bad," he says to finalize his answer.

There are sixteen of us in the audience. Most are in pods of three to four family members or friends. Two people in the audience are bald, and I am wondering if they will be recipients. Several people raise their hands to ask questions. One of the bald persons asks the next question: "What is the donating environment like? Is it sterile?"

The donor says, "The actual room where they did my peripheral donation is just an isolated room off the main area of the blood bank where other people are donating blood. The room has a recliner and a small TV screen on an arm for entertainment. Otherwise the room is bare except for the equipment, which is a computer and a machine that takes up a good portion of one wall. Everything seemed sterile and clean, and you are in a separate room."

"What is it like? Does it hurt?"

"I can walk you through what I remember." He talks while looking up, envisioning what happened. "I sat in the recliner, and there was a technician who is skilled in the whole process who looked at the veins in my arms while I was squeezing foam balls in each palm. He seemed happy and told me I had 'good veins.'" This draws a few laughs. "He cleaned the skin with a scrubbing device and then numbed the skin over a vein on each arm with a little injection that feels 'like a bee sting.' I could feel the next, larger needle go in; it wasn't painful, but I could feel the girth of the needle."

He continues to look up as he tells the whole story from memory. "There was specialized tubing which pulled the blood into two cylindrical pumps, and then a whirling circular area or centrifuge, and then the blood was drawn out by two more cylindrical pumps. Some of the blood filtered into two different bags, one of which was the stem cells. About three other bags of clear IV fluid bags serve to help thin the blood and keep things flowing. Then I had a second IV in the other arm, for the return of the blood from the machine. The computer, as best I could tell, has a way of tracking the progress."

"What was the hardest part?"

"It just took a long time, about five to six hours, and I was stuck in a recliner. There was a TV to watch, and the controller was easy to access. I also had a button to call the technician, in case he stepped away at any point."

"What do you do if you have to use the bathroom?"

"Yeah, about that, I remember my helper telling me, 'You will not be able to get up, and so I recommend that you try to go to the bathroom before we get started. Once you are hooked up, if you really need to go, I'll help you with this,' and he held up a plastic urinal."

We all laugh.

"Is it always a male attendant?" a lady asks.

"I think they try to match a male to males and a female to females."

"What do the ladies use?" A woman questions the urinal.

"I am not entirely certain, but I think a bedpan."

"Did you have to go?" someone asks laughingly.

"They let you drink liquids, but not eat. I tried not to ask for a drink, because I was sure that then I would need to pee, but I couldn't help it. I got desperately thirsty. I think when you see blood leaving your body, it triggers some thirst mechanism, so I had some juice. Then of course I had to pee, and I tried to hold it. I even tried to take a nap, but there was no point, given that I had to pee. I broke down and called the attendant, who made it seem as normal as can be to help someone urinate." He develops a funny grimace.

We are all laughing.

"How long did it take?"

"Six hours, as advertised."

"What was the recovery like?"

"When I was done, I walked to the waiting area, where there was a refrigerator full of juices and water and a counter full of cookies and snacks. I could have also ordered a meal from the cafeteria, but I opted not to. I stayed in the waiting area, maybe an hour, probably less. I just had to drink lots of liquids the next few days and not do any heavy lifting or exercise, especially with my arms, for the next day or so. I didn't really notice a difference. I think they take less blood out for a stem cell donation than they do for a usual blood donation."

Once he gets past the recovery, there are only a few more questions.

"How is your sister doing?" I ask.

"Well, she got the donation just three days ago, so she's still in the hospital, but so far so good," he affirms.

The group has kind words of encouragement before disassembling. I can't say that I had my questions answered, but I did get a sense of the reality and the necessity of the experience.

HLA typing...

We meet with the ID doctor and the hematologist again in family conference room 3A; the closest such room to the isolation unit. Essentially they started my screening with something called HLA typing to see if I would even be a match for Hope. I am not entirely sure what this means, and so I ask.

The ID doctor motions to the hematologist, who explains, "HLA stands for human leukocyte antigen. Leukocytes are white blood cells, and we need to match the donor and the recipient as best as we can because otherwise your white blood cells will attack Hope's white blood cells and/or other tissues."

I guess I was thinking that children have immature white blood cells and that they accept almost any donor blood or tissue. But I gather from what he is saying that it is my blood that may not accept being in Hope's system and could attack her. Wait, is that right?

The hematologist continues as if reading my mind, "Yes, your blood cells, the leukocytes, could attack Hope, and not just her blood cells, but all of her; this is what we call graft-versus-host disease, or GVHD."

The ID doctor breaks in with, "Amazingly, you are a pretty good match."

"But, not perfect," states the hematologist.

"Well, it's still pretty amazing, miraculous even," the ID doctor pipes in.

Then at this point they discuss how many antigens or alleles are matching and whether it is enough. I am thinking that alleles must mean the same thing as antigens, and that antigens must mean the same as proteins, as discussed by the coordinator. I keep hoping they will say how many of the six I matched, but they do not talk in such easy to digest language. From what I understand, perhaps I am not the best match, but I will do.

The hematologist states, "The best possible circumstance would be immature stem cells derived from a placental or an umbilical source. Such cells would decrease the risk of GVHD, and Hope, also being newborn and with an immature immune system, already has a decreased risk of rejecting such stem cells."

The ID doctor, then, argues that won't help the fact that such cells would not lack the CCR5 receptor, and that Hope has HIV and doesn't seem to tolerate medicines well.

The hematologist clarifies, "Umbilical stem cells that *also* lack the CCR5 receptor." He contemplates aloud, "I am not sure if anyone has thought of checking the CCR5 status of umbilical stem cell donations. Even just testing such stem cells from Caucasians would be cost prohibitive, being that only one percent of Caucasians lacks the CCR5 receptor at best."

The ID doctor, following his train of thought, states, "Yes, but weighing that cost against a lifetime of HIV medicines..." He is staring up as if trying to calculate it all in his head, but then refocuses his gaze and abruptly responds. "Yes, well, this is all conjecture, interesting though, but, of course, this is not reality. The reality is that we have you as a stem cell donor and that of the ten alleles, the antigens that really matter all miraculously match."

"Ten," I think. "What happened to six?"

"Yes, yes, we have gone over that point before, which is why we are here to discuss your"—the hematologist directs to me—"donating stem cells to Hope."

I accept by saying, "I will do whatever you think is necessary."

The hematologist informs me that there are two methods to donate stem cells. One is a small surgery where they make a hole in my hip bone and withdraw marrow, which is the source of stem cells. The second way is to receive injections of a medicine to help mobilize stem cells into my blood stream. The injections are daily for four to five days, and on the last day, I would have blood pulled from a vein through a machine that would isolate and filter out the stem cells, and then the remaining blood would be returned to my body.

I remember the video that explained both options to me in detail, and so I nod with understanding.

At this point the ID doctor states that he read a scientific article that reports that bone marrow–derived stem cells were better accepted in cases like Hope's.

The hematologist rebukes that it was a small study, maybe only fifty patients total. He is also uncertain that those cases were like Hope's. "Furthermore, there have not been any good, randomized prospective trials because no one wants to risk showing that the peripheral stem cell method causes more graft-versus-host disease, or GVHD. After considering the risk that the peripheral stem cell method has a greater likelihood of causing GVHD, I have decided that the bone marrow–derived stem cell method is probably the best option for Hope."

The ID doctor starts to mention another study, where bone marrow that was once frozen also cut down on graft-versus-host disease, when the hematologist interrupts, "I didn't realize that you read up so much on stem cell transplants."

"I have a particular interest in this case," the ID doctor admits sheepishly and with a little frustration.

The hematologist then takes over and says, "I suggest a bone marrow donation that will be frozen. Almost all stem cell donations are frozen, as it is unlikely to deliver the cells so rapidly as to not require freezing, but in this case we will also freeze the donation so that it might cut down on graft-versus-host disease. Please know that a few studies have hinted that freezing cuts down on GVHD, but it is not certain. Also know that Hope is at high risk for GVHD, being that she is so young, an infant."

If there is anything I can do to increase baby Hope's chance of survival, then I will do it for her and my sister. "Can you tell me a little more about graft-versus-host disease?" I inquire.

"The donor's cells attack and kill the recipient from the inside out. Sometimes we can manage the symptoms and halt the progress, and the person can go on living with mild symptoms of say, diarrhea, dry eyes, and rashes; other times it's deadly, attacking vital organs, the heart, the lungs, and the liver," the hematologist replies.

I nod slowly with trepidation from better understanding.

After we have all agreed to the hematologist's plan, he dismisses the meeting.

The next day I visit with the coordinator, who I anxiously await to critique her attire. She seems to like the army boots, and today she wears them with bright purple tights and a black leather skirt. Unexpectedly, she has a purple paisley top that actually matches the outfit, including her dark purple lipstick. The oddity in her outfit is a black leather dog collar. I make no exaggeration; the collar is suited for a dog, with a metal loop that has a red, shiny metallic heart tag. I really want to look more closely at the tag. Could it really be a rabies vaccination tag?

She beams at me and calls me "the miracle man." I assume she's referring to the rare chance that I actually did match. She directs me into an exam room as before. Typing in more information, she asks me if I want to be on the stem cell donor registry.

I realize this would mean that in the future, if I matched another individual, I could be contacted to donate more stem cells. This is a nationwide registry, and so I believe that my cells could go to anyone in need in the nation. There is a part of me that would love to donate to others, and I think that I would be a great donor, especially in certain circumstances. The reality, though, is that I cannot get just anyone's full consent with full disclosure to donate, and so I must decline.

The coordinator looks slightly disappointed but then shrugs. "You are at the upper age limit"—she confirms my age—"which is forty-six." This alarms me to know that in less than one year, I cannot be a stem cell donor. As I am wondering why, she continues, "I've been on the registry six years, and I haven't been a match for anyone yet, which just proves that I am unique!"

"Yes, you are," I agree.

She draws three more full tubes of blood. Then she directs the computer screen toward me and tells me that I will need to answer the screen-directed questions. She leaves and closes the door.

"Click here to begin your questions."—"Click"

"Are you over eighteen years of age?" —Yes

"Are you in good health?"

I freeze in shock. Am I about to face the social questions, which I so dread? Why wait until this point to ask these questions? Maybe it is better that I was not expecting this; I had no time to worry about it. My mouth is dry, and I sit there looking at the screen; getting started is the hardest part. Slowly my mind begins to thaw; I remind myself that I have my sister's consent. My sister is a doctor and Hope's mom, and she thinks that I am Hope's best chance at living. My stem cells are known to resist HIV, and, somehow, I have made it this far. The odds were greatly stacked against me to be a match for Hope, but the HLA typing shows that I am a good match for donating stem cells to her. I am the "miracle man!"

I pep myself up as much as I can, repeating "miracle man" in my head a few times. I am most encouraged by the fact that I have my sister's consent, and I begin to answer the questions slowly, but with purpose. After the first few questions, I pick up speed and go through them amazingly fast, not giving myself time to think about the answers. I give the correct answers, the needed answers, the truthful answers regarding the last five years of my life.

When I have completed the questions, I open the door. Soon the coordinator returns with a gown and a drape, which she places on the exam table. She tells me to undress to my underwear, to take off any jewelry, and to leave the gown open in the front, which makes it easier to do the EKG. Then she leaves once more.

In a few moments, a man enters the room with a rolling laptop. He introduces himself as the EKG technician. He asks me to lie flat and breathe normally. I immediately focus on my breathing, until I feel the cold, cold gel electrodes he places on various parts of my body. He reminds me to breathe normally while he obtains my EKG. The laptop produces heart tracings on red graph paper. He holds this up and looks satisfied. He tells me that I can remove the electrodes, and he places the trash bin next to the bed. I peel off the gel adhesives while he knocks on a door that I had not noticed before. It seems that between this and another exam room, there is a small adjoining X-ray room.

A lady opens the door and asks me to step inside. She introduces herself as the X-ray technician. She instructs me where to stand. I have to face front and hold my breath, and then I have to turn to the side and hold my breath. Once the chest X-rays are complete, she directs me back to my exam room and tells me that a physician will review the EKG and chest X-ray and then will be in shortly to perform a physical exam.

The physician asks me how I have been feeling. He says he has gone over my past medical history on the computer and asks if there are any changes or if there is anything that I would like to discuss. I reply that I am fine, and I have no changes and nothing to discuss. With that, he begins the exam.

Before leaving the room, he tells me that I can put my clothes back on.

A few moments later, the coordinator steps back inside. She tells me that I am done for today and that if everything goes well, that in a few days she will call me to set up the surgery. I will need to meet the surgeon in his or her office, where the surgeon will review my records, go over the consent forms for surgery, and set a date for the surgery. She hands me a list of surgeons and tells me that if I have a preference, to call and tell her; otherwise, she just picks a surgeon in a rotating fashion.

She smiles with dark lips, says I'll be hearing from her, and tells me I am free to go.

Wow, I had all of that done, and it's not even lunchtime yet!

I understand now how she gets along with the hematologist and that she must be highly valued. If the efficiency of the clinic is due to the coordinator, then every doctor's office needs a coordinator just like her!

When I return to Hope's room, my sister looks haggard and depressed. She tells me last night was busy on the unit with alarms and teams rushing in and out. The child next door died.

"You just missed the last of the family coming to say good-bye, and then the child..." She breaks down and can't go on.

Life on the unit is difficult, and I sense a bit of desperation in my sister. This is not the first time a child has died since we have been here. One day while we were returning from lunch, we were unable to get back on the unit for several hours because of similar circumstances. Daily we see bald children who look quite frail; occasionally the luster is completely gone. Some of the families have gotten to know one another. We have gotten to know a few of the families and a few of the children's names. Everyone is polite and kind enough not to ask about medical conditions unless such information is given. My sister is known as the person who knows the area, the person to ask where to buy anything or to ask which restaurants, especially pizza and Chinese, deliver to the hospital.

As advertised, five days later, the coordinator calls me. She tells me the surgeon's name, clinic location, and phone number. I have an appointment to meet her tomorrow. The surgery will be the following Monday, but I should firm that up at the appointment. She tells me that the surgery will be in the main ORs because they are closer to hematology-pathologists and the blood bank.

On the list there were six potential surgeons, two had female-sounding names. My sister did not know any of the surgeons to offer a recommendation, but when I tell her which surgeon I will be meeting, she says, "Oh, I've heard that she's good!"

I want to ask my sister what she has heard about this surgeon, but I sense she would respond with the generic, "Just that she's good!"

I ask my sister if she would like to come with me to meet the surgeon, but I know that after the last child died, my sister has been reluctant to leave Hope's side for much of anything.

The next day, I find my way to the surgeon's office. The waiting room is a dark green and has pictures of hounds in hunting poses in clusters on the walls. The receptionist has me sign in and hands me a clipboard with forms to fill out. Some forms do not seem to pertain to me, but I fill them out as best as I can.

"Who referred you?" —The blood stem cell coordinator

"Have you been told you need a surgery? —Yes

"If so, which surgery?" —Bone marrow stem cell removal

"Have you been having pain?" —No

"If so, where do you hurt?" —NA

I answer NA to almost the whole page of questions.

Until I reach the last question: "How do you hope that we can help you today?"

I draw an arrow all the way back up to my response of, "Bone marrow stem cell removal."

The next two pages of questions are titled, "review of systems." The questions remind me of the five pages of questions I filled out the first day that I met the stem cell coordinator. There are similar subheadings: respiratory, cardiac, gastrointestinal...neurology. I briefly look at the questions and mark, "no," and then extend a line down through all of the no answers.

The fourth page pertains mostly to medications.

The fifth page pertains to any prior surgeries, mobility issues, prosthetics, and/or metal in the body.

The sixth page asks if I have a living will.

The seventh page is for next of kin, who to notify, and release of medical information.

The eighth and ninth pages are regarding patient confidentiality.

The tenth and eleventh pages are regarding patients' rights.

Initially, I assumed that the stack of papers on the clipboard were to serve multiple people. I would have never guessed that the entire stack was for me.

When I get through all of the papers on the clipboard, I return them to the receptionist, who scans and shreds each form. She then confirms with me that I am here for a stem cell donation and that all costs will be referred to the recipient. She tells me that she has all that information, but that she will still need a copy of my driver's license. Once she has scanned this into the system, she returns my card and asks me to have a seat.

A patient wheels into the waiting room, and the receptionist waves the patient and the person pushing the wheelchair directly to the back.

In ten to fifteen minutes, I am directed from the waiting room to the doctor's office. Her office is typical: wood desk, desk chair and two consultant chairs, and many diplomas.

In about five minutes, the doctor enters and introduces herself. From the desk chair, she pulls up my file on the computer. "You appear to be in good health. Have you been having any problems lately?"

"No."

"Just a few questions. Do you have any heart problems?'

"No."

"Have you ever needed to take antibiotics at the dentist's office?"

"No."

"Have you ever been told that you have a heart murmur?"

"No."

"Have you ever had asthma or had any allergic reaction to any medications?"

"No."

"Are you on any medicines that you forgot to put on any of the forms, such as testosterone gel or any diet pills or energy pills or liquids, even if they are over-the-counter?" She looks at me expectantly.

"No."

"Great, I love hearing no!" She brightens. "All right, then I am going to go over the consent form for the procedure, and then I will do a brief physical exam. Lastly, my nurse will give you surgery instructions."

She pulls out a multipage form and begins, "This says that you are going to have a bone marrow aspiration. I will do what's in your best interest. Should any difficulty arise, I will do my best to do whatever is necessary. You will require anesthesia. The anesthesiologists will have forms for you to sign on the day of the procedure, but in general, the risks of anesthesia are as follows." She lists the risks, including death, and then she says, "Initial here."

Whoa, all right; I initial.

"If there were an emergency, would you accept blood?"

"Yes."

"The risks of a blood transfusion are transfusion reaction, kidney failure, heart failure, anemia, hepatitis, HIV, and death. Initial here."

Don't think, just initial.

"Lastly, the risks of bone marrow aspiration are bleeding, infection, bone pain, and death."

On the third time hearing death, I have to ask, "Has anyone ever died from this procedure?"

She pauses and looks up from the paper. "I can't say no one ever, but no one that I am aware of."

I initial and sign.

Next she directs me into an exam room, where a nurse asks me to undress to my underwear and put on a paper gown. In a short while, the nurse knocks, reenters, and proceeds to take my weight and asks my height. She tells me to have a seat on the exam table and takes my blood pressure.

In a few moments the doctor reenters the exam room. She has me look up and open my mouth. Then she reports, "No dental prosthetics. OP normal." The nurse enters data into the computer. The doctor feels my neck and reports, "No lymph nodes; supple." She pulls a stethoscope from the wall and listens to my heart and lungs and says, "RRR; lungs clear." She wraps the stethoscope around her neck and asks me to lay flat. She feels my belly, first lightly and then with pressure and states, "No palpable masses, no triple A." She taps over areas of my stomach. "No enlarged spleen or liver." Next she places the stethoscope to my neck and asks me to hold my breath. "No bruits." Then directed to me, she says, "Okay, you can breathe now." Next she places the stethoscope to both sides of my groin, which is chilling and unexpected, then behind my knees. "Again, no bruits." She palpates the tops of my feet and behind my inner ankles. "Normal and equal peripheral pulses." Further she dictates, "Normal skin, no clubbing, no cyanosis, no edema, normal gait." Then directed to me, she says, "Which I noted on the way to the room."

The doctor looks at me. "Do you have any questions?"

"No."

"I love no!" she repeats warmly. "We are going to leave, and you can get dressed, then my nurse will return with instructions." She smiles and leaves.

Other than the time and place to meet for surgery, my only instructions are not to eat or drink anything after midnight before the surgery. Before leaving, the nurse hands me a card and tells me to call if anything unexpected arises or if I have any questions or concerns.

That evening, I speak to my sister about my plans to go home, to my job and my life. I will stay the full twelve weeks, of which I am nearing the end, but then I must go back to work.

She tells me she understands.

I ask her who will watch Hope when she needs to go back to work.

"I guess I have been negligent on finding someone to help with Hope. First I have to get Hope out of the hospital. I guess I was waiting to see when or if that would happen."

"Nothing is quite certain," I acknowledge, "but I think you should ask mom for help."

She just stares down at the floor.

"It's time to tell her. I can't think of anyone else who can help you when you need to go back to work. I propose that this weekend we must have our powwow."

The powwow...

The Saturday night before my surgery, I arrange for the family to come over for dinner at my sister's house. I have been known to cook a good meal, and I am surprised that I haven't thought of doing this earlier. My sister knows that I will prompt her to tell my parents everything, and she prepares a cocktail for herself. I have also bought a few bottles of wine for the occasion.

When we sit for dinner, I propose a toast. "Mom, you said that we would always love and take care of Hope, who will always be a part of our family. I would like to raise a glass to Hope Angela and to her health."

We take a sip of wine, and my sister looks a little relieved.

"I also wanted us to get together because, as you know, the doctors plan to give Hope a stem cell transplant, and we are all hoping that this will help her to be able to come home and live a normal and healthy life."

I guess everyone thinks this is another toast, as my dad says, "Here, here," and we all take another sip.

My mom can't keep quiet for long, and she asks, "Do the doctors even know what happened to Hope? I mean, what caused all of this? She has been in the hospital for a very long time."

I look at my sister and wait for her to respond.

"Mom and Dad," she begins, "we...I want to tell you about Hope." She looks at me. "Hope's mom had HIV and died from pneumonia, but she passed the infection on to Hope."

My mom is looking upset, and I sense that she thinks maybe my sister didn't know this before the adoption and she will say something about her being duped and that we can get a lawyer and reverse the adoption or something inappropriate. So I quickly say, "We are sorry that we kept this from you, and it may be hard to realize that someone would *want* to adopt a child with HIV." I emphasize want.

"Yes, I wanted Hope, regardless of whether she had HIV or not," my sister confirms. She tells the story of how Hope's mom died. "Truthfully, she did die of pneumonia, but she also had HIV. Finding the right home for the child would have been tricky." She tells how she has wanted a child for such a long time and how this all seemed to fall into place. Then she tells of Hope's medicines. "They caused Hope to spit up everywhere and retch her poor little esophagus raw. She bled in her vomit, and then they found out her blood counts dropped such that she now needs a stem cell transplant. We really are not entirely sure why her cell counts have dropped, but there's been no improvement off of the medicines."

My sister seems worn out from the whole situation; we all sympathize with her.

Then she directs the conversation to me and says that miraculously my partner died of HIV, while I did not, so that's why I chose to be a stem cell donor for Hope. Maybe if my stem cells are in Hope, then she too will reject HIV.

My dad seems to get this immediately and seems amazed.

My mom is dumbfounded and asks many questions for clarity. I am proud of her not asking my sister why, why in the world, she would take on such a child.

As my sister makes my mom understand everything, I opt to serve dinner.

Before we are finished, I ask my parents to help my sister, as I will need to get back to my job, and at some point my sister will need to get back to her job.

"Yes, yes, I will watch little Hope for you," my mom answers with certainty.

"You won't go telling all of your friends, either, right?" my dad surprisingly admonishes.

"No, no. Just let me know how I can help." She confirms and then adds, "I knew you two were hiding something. I just knew it."

Our dinner is a success. I know that my mom could have made a comment like, "What were you thinking?" And I know that my sister could have said something like, "You never support me." Instead, we are a family.

The surgery...

Hearing about my surgery, my parents volunteer to drive me to the hospital, and they sit in the waiting room during my procedure and hospital recovery. This makes me nervous because my mom may not be able to keep her mouth shut. Likely she will "befriend" some poor soul in the waiting room and tell them all about me and my surgery and Hope.

On the drive to the hospital, I sternly tell my mother that I do not give her permission to discuss my surgery or Hope or anything with anyone! I also dictate for my dad to keep watch over her and not let her ramble; furthermore, he is not to disappear behind a newspaper.

My mom looks a little taken aback and replies, "I wouldn't say."

Interjecting, my dad confirms, "No, you will not."

"Just don't say anything," I reemphasize.

When we arrive at the hospital, it is quite early, but as we near the surgical area, the place is bustling with energy. Many personnel circle around with clipboards. Their elbows stick out, reminding me of wings on moths fluttering around the bright, white fluorescent lights.

I sign in, and I am directed to "preop," where a staff member meets me and directs me to a stretcher, number "8." She confirms my name and places a plastic identity wristband on my arm. There is a gown, and as she points to it, I know exactly what to do. She pulls curtains, and I undress, put on the gown, and place my items into a clear plastic bag. I peek through the curtains, and she confirms that I am "ready."

I lie down and pull up the sheet. She pulls up two plastic chairs for my parents to sit alongside the bed. She takes my vital signs and asks if I have to go to the bathroom before she places an IV.

Suddenly, I do have to go to the bathroom, so I get up, trying to keep myself as concealed as possible. I instinctively draw the back of my gown closed, holding it with one hand, and I make my way to the restroom.

Once I return, I lie back on stretcher number "8," again with some effort to not expose myself.

My helper returns and verifies my signatures on the surgical consents. Then she looks over my arms, picks out a ropey vein, and with dexterity places an IV. She draws two tubes of blood, which she places on the bed next to my arm; she connects the IV tubing and secures the line with tape. Next she picks up the two tubes of blood, places stickers on them, and disappears.

As if possessing the ability to sense blood, two individuals appear at the bedside and introduce themselves as the anesthesiologist and the certified registered nurse anesthetist, or CRNA. The anesthesiologist tells me the CRNA will go over the consents and walk me back to surgery, but not to worry, he will be there when I go to sleep and awaken. With that, the tall doctor takes his leave.

The CRNA is a young lady who has a sweet face. She wears a surgical cap with martini decorations and holds a clipboard, more consent papers.

As I am signing my life away, my surgeon arrives. She asks me how I am feeling and if I have any questions. I respond that I am as well as can be expected and that I am ready.

The surgeon gets the approval of the CRNA to go back to the OR and then releases the break of the bed. The surgeon tells my parents that she will find them and speak with them as soon as she is done. With this, a staff member comes to escort my parents to the waiting room.

The CRNA is holding a syringe and tells me that she will give me a "little IV cocktail" on the way to the OR. My parents leave, and I vaguely remember reminding my parents to keep their mouths shut. Then on the way to the OR, I tell the CRNA that maybe she should have chosen a different cap, because she wouldn't want patients thinking she's an alcoholic or anything, especially with referring to IV cocktails. I slur all the way to the OR.

I dreamily remember moving to another bed, bright lights, and a voice telling me to imagine a calm beach scene.

As if my eyes had just fluttered and I dozed off momentarily, the next thing I remember is people saying my name. I am uncertain that I am even asleep, but I do not want to be disturbed. Whatever this twilight state is, leave me alone.

Eventually, I feel hip pain, which brings me back to my senses. I moan in pain.

"Are you in pain?" someone surmises. "Would you like something for pain?"

"Um-hum," I groan.

Then I am out again.

Again, I hear voices calling my name. I rouse enough to know that I am no longer in the OR; I am on a stretcher, parked in another large room. The surgeon materializes at my bedside. She reports everything went well, and she is confident she got a good sample.

All of this is very surreal. Somehow I am taken by wheelchair to my parents' car, and the next thing I remember, I am waking up, lying on my parents' couch with a towel that my mom placed to catch my drool.

My parents watch over me for a few days. My mom cooks meals and monitors my pain medicines. By the third day, I barely need any pain medicines, and I am sick of being babied. My mom chides me that I am not allowed to drive if I need pain medicines, and she threatens to hide the prescription bottles.

I look at my dad, who rolls his eyes and then offers to drive me wherever I need to go.

My dad drives me to the hospital, where after I check in on Hope, I plan to take my sister's car and stay at her place again. Seeing Hope and my sister, that they are both stable, is a welcomed sight. While I visit, I have a few realizations. If Hope gets well, then my mom's helping with her care will be a blessing for my mom, who needs to nurture others. Likewise, Hope will also be a blessing for my dad, who could probably use a little less supervision. Lastly, I love my parents, but I am content to be gay.

After this, we are just waiting for the day that Hope gets the stem cells. My day-to-day life returns, as I have come to know it at the hospital, visiting Hope and my sister in isolation.

Hope's cell counts are alarmingly low, but somehow, she remains stable in the isolation wing for the time being. We all pray that she does not contract any infections while we wait for her stem cell transplant.

Resiliency

The day Hope is set to get the stem cells, my sister and I web-call my parents so they can also take part.

The ID doctor and hematologist are present when the stem cells arrive. Two medical personnel arrive with a small cooler. They open the cooler and confirm that the ID on the bag inside matches the ID band on Hope's ankle; they need another witness, so the hematologist also takes part. They verbally call out numbers and visually inspect the bag and Hope's band. They hang the bag on an IV pole and connect the tubing.

The hematologist nods and says brightly, "Well, this is it." Then he clasps his hands, bows his head, and appears to pray briefly.

Reflexively, I bow my head and think, "Oh please, God, let this all go well. Let this be Hope's last treatment. Let her be well." My sister seems to have her hands clasped, and although I can't see my parents, I am betting that they are similarly praying.

The stem cell transplant, the actual event, is anticlimactic; just a small bag of fluid drains into her IV. The bag is slightly layered: yellow on top of orange on top of red, which almost resembles a sunrise. The idea of a bag of sunshine makes me smile, but otherwise, there's no real fanfare and no immediate result.

We are silent, but my mom can't help herself. "Is that it? Are those the stem cells?"

The hematologist steps toward the computer and assures her that the bag has my stem cells and that Hope is getting them. He nods in approval and then steps out of the room.

My mom and dad look anxious but hold any further comments until the bag has drained and is disconnected.

The ID doctor watches and then wishes us all well. He leaves shortly afterward.

One nurse stays to monitor Hope for a while. She informs us that Hope's pulse and oxygen levels will continue to be monitored electronically. She points to the monitor on the wall, and then she disappears.

We are left watching and waiting with an expectation of uncertainty.

After a short while, we close our web-call, and the day continues to go by as most other days in the last month or two.

Only over the next days to weeks do we realize that something miraculous has taken place.

Hope's improvement is remarkable. Once she meets criteria to leave the isolation ward, I decide to return home. I am conflicted to leave before Hope is discharged from the hospital, but with the way she is progressing, I know she won't be in the hospital for much longer. Hope has only faint signs of old bruises, she is gaining weight, and more importantly, her blood counts are ever rising.

My bags are packed, and I drive my sister's car to the hospital.

The sunlight streams into the window. My sister sits on a vinyl-covered couch, looking calm and contented. She sees me enter the room with my bags and gives a warm but heavyhearted smile. In turn, I realize the stress of the last few months: a late night call about an orphaned baby, a reconnection with an old lawyer friend, an adoption, a box of ashes, a critically ill baby, an uncle, and an improbable stem cell donation.

She comes over to me and gives me an enormous hug and says, "Thank you, thank you, thank you. I love you."

My eyes fill with tears. "I am going to miss you, but I'll visit soon, and we can visit by computer in between."

She releases me and wipes a tear away.

I look into the bassinette to say good-bye to Hope Angela. As I peer at her, she looks at me with bright shining eyes and then presents a beautiful smile.

My sister is standing near and radiantly exclaims, "Oh my goodness! Her first smile!"

I laugh and grab Hope's feet and give them a raspberry. Hope responds with a full belly laugh. I am elated, soaring even. We laugh with Hope, for her response reassures us that she is well. Hope has lightened my good-bye, my heart, and my spirit.

Before leaving, I respond, "Thank you, thank you, thank you! I love you!"

www.ingramcontent.com/pod-product-compliance
Lightning Source LLC
Chambersburg PA
CBHW060054150626
46556CB00017BA/651